About the Author

Well, what can I say about me? I'm twenty-nine, married and a mother to one. I work full time, and when I'm not spending time with my family or friends, you can find me either reading or on my laptop writing.

After spending god knows how much money on my reading obsession (yes, I can admit I'm a little obsessed), I decided to give writing my own book a try. I still can't believe someone thought it was good enough to publish. I'm certainly not going to argue with them.

I hope you enjoy reading my work as much as I enjoyed writing it.

Webpage:
www.tonigriffin.net

Blog:
www.tonigriffin.blogspot.com

Facebook:
http://www.facebook.com/?sk=nf#!/toni.griffin.author

HOLLAND BROTHERS

VOLUME TWO

TONI GRIFFIN

Published by Silver Publishing
Publisher of Erotic Romance

SILVER PUBLISHING

ISBN 978-1-61495-355-5

Holland Brothers 1: Protective Mate
Holland Brothers 2: Forbidden Mate

Editor: Jason Huffman
Cover Artist: Reese Dante

Visit Silver Publishing at https://spsilverpublishing.com

Note from the Publisher

Dear Reader,

Thank you for your purchase of this title. The authors and staff of Silver Publishing hope you enjoy this read and that we will have a long and happy association together.

Please remember that the only money authors make from writing comes from the sales of their books. If you like their work, spread the word and tell others about the books, but please refrain from copying this book in any form. Authors depend on sales and sales only to support their families.

If you see "free shares" offered or cut-rate sales on ebook pirate sites of this title, you can report the offending entry to copyright@spsilverpublishing.com

Thank you for not pirating our titles.

Lodewyk Deysel
Publisher
Silver Publishing
http://www.spsilverpublishing.com

PROTECTIVE MATE
HOLLAND BROTHERS, BOOK THREE

Within the space of two years Zack lost nearly everyone that had ever meant anything to him. After his parents were killed in a car accident and his best friend succumbed to cancer, Zack is left alone with only his eighteen month old daughter. Her ultra-religious and homophobic grandparents will do anything they can to take his daughter away from him. To stop this, Zack packs up and moves to a small town in northern Victoria.

Simon has known he was gay since he was fifteen and he had resigned himself to never being a father. Walking into his house one afternoon, he is shocked to find not only his mate, but a two year old calling his mate daddy.

Is Simon ready to be a father? Can Zack open his heart after so much hurt and risk loving someone else?

PROTECTIVE

Mate

THE HOLLAND BROTHERS, BOOK 3

TONI GRIFFIN

SILVER PUBLISHING
Published by Silver Publishing
Publisher of Erotic Romance

Dedication

To my new nephew, James—May your life be filled with love and joy
for many years to come.

And to my brothers and the women that love them. Thank you for your support

Trademarks Acknowledgement

The author acknowledges the trademarked status and trademark owners of the following wordmarks mentioned in this work of fiction:

Toyota Camry: Toyota Motor Corporation
iPod: Apple Computer, Inc.
Nike: Nike, Inc.

CHAPTER 1

"Daddy?" Zack looked in the rear-view mirror at the most important person in his life. His daughter sat in her booster seat surrounded by everything they owned.

"Yes, Pumpkin?" Zack constantly flicked his eyes back and forth between his precious cargo and the road ahead.

"Are we there yet?" Zack sighed. The question had been constant for the last several hours. It had to be hard for Hayley. Within the space of a six month period, she lost the mother she loved, the house she grew up in and was being taken from the day care she knew and friends she loved. To top everything off, her grandparents were trying to take her away from her father, so he'd finally left with Hayley to start over in a new town with new people and hopefully new friends.

"Not yet Hayley, but soon okay? We'll find the motel and unpack the car, and then we'll find a nice park where you can play for a little while. How does that sound?" The squeals of delight from the backseat let Zack know Hayley was onboard with the park idea.

Glancing back again, Zack couldn't believe how much she looked like her mother. Her sparkling jade green eyes and the cutest little button nose you had ever seen, above a small mouth with rose pink lips, reminded him daily of the only woman he'd ever loved. But her best feature Zack thought, the only feature she got from her father, fell past her shoulders in loose, bright auburn ringlets. One of Sarah's favourite things before she passed was to brush Hayley's hair.

Zack felt momentarily overwhelmed with grief at the thought of his best friend. On their first day in high school, Zack and Sarah had both gone to sit in the same seat at lunch, neither of them paying any attention to their surroundings, and ended up best friends by the time the bell rang to signify lunch was over.

Their high school years seemed to fly past with the two sharing everything. Zack confided in Sarah when he realised the boys at their school held more appeal to him than the girls. Sarah had hugged him and kissed him on the cheek and said being gay didn't matter and she would always love him. She'd encouraged Zack to talk to his parents and let them know what was going on with him. His mum had surprised him and said she'd suspected for a while and his dad nodded and said as long as Zack was happy then that was all he cared about. Zack had hugged his parents, never more thankful for their support.

Sarah however, kept the knowledge from her parents until after they'd graduated from high school and moved into an apartment together. Her parents, being the religious, god fearing people they were, were adamant Sarah have nothing further to do with him. When she refused, they informed her God would punish her for association with *him.*

Who knows what Sarah's parents would have thought if they ever found out he was a werewolf as well as identifying as gay. They'd probably keel over in an apoplectic fit. Zack chuckled at that idea and thought back to when Sarah found out he was a werewolf. The first full moon after Zack turned sixteen he and Sarah were lying on the floor in the lounge at his place, doing their homework. Zack's entire body had heated, like his blood was boiling, then his arms started sprouting fur. He'd looked over at Sarah, saw her wide eyes staring back at him and said the only thing he could think of. "Please don't scream."

Her eyes had widened even further at his words then his bones started to reshape, his face elongated and before he knew it, he stood on all fours tangled in his jeans and shirt and staring at his best friend as she looked back at him in wide-eyed shock.

Zack's mother had come through from the kitchen

clearly in the middle of asking them a question when she noticed Zack and stopped in her tracks, mouth open. She quickly looked at Sarah and regained her senses. "Sarah, honey, are you okay?"

"That is so fricken cool!" Sarah turned and quickly picked up her homework before waving it in front of Zack's face. "Come on Zack! Be a good boy and eat this for me. That way I don't have to do it and I'll have such a good excuse." She giggled as Zack took a playful bite at her hand before his mother scolded him. She sent him sent to his room until he could change back so she could talk to Sarah.

Sarah tried to get him to eat her homework several more times after that and when they moved in together, she came home one day with a collar and lead and hung them by the door. She'd laughed herself silly then ran to the toilet before she wet herself the first time Zack saw the items.

Pulling himself out of his memories, Zack once again looked into the mirror and noticed his daughter was now fast asleep, her favourite toy, a plush wolf, held close to her chest. Concentrating on the road ahead, Zack wondered what he was going to do without his best friend. Sarah had been a constant in his life for thirteen years. When Sarah received her diagnosis of cancer, the news hit the friends like a tonne of bricks. They went to sleep that night wrapped in each other's arms, both with red rimmed eyes and tear streaked faces.

Sarah woke him up the next day by asking for his sperm. After the initial shock wore off, Zack had agreed. The doctors gave her a maximum of two years to live and wanted to start treatments right way; they didn't expect to be able to prolong her life by years, only months. Sarah had wanted to be a mother more than anything else in the world. Any treatment she undertook would take that opportunity away from her.

Zack couldn't deny his best friend anything, and as he was gay he never expected to have a child, but he couldn't think of anyone he would rather have one with. Knowing a part of Sarah would live on in their daughter, helped Zack with the loss of his friend.

After long discussions and more tears, they spoke with Zack's parents. The couple were overjoyed to find out they would have a grandchild. With Zack being an only child and gay, they had resigned themselves to having no grandkids. His parents were so happy they offered to pay for Sarah's wish to come true. Zack and Sarah were extremely grateful for their help, as all Sarah's parents said, upon hearing the news of their daughter's illness, was she would be punished for her association with Zack.

They were lucky and Sarah got pregnant on the first attempt. Zack could see the strain the pregnancy put on Sarah, but she never complained. She worked as much as possible to help pay for her share of the expenses, no matter how much Zack tried to tell her to slow down and take it easy.

Sarah was about 6 months pregnant when Zack received the phone call one night to tell him his parents had been involved in a car accident. They'd been driving back from his dad's Christmas party when the driver of a semi trailer had fallen asleep at the wheel and crossed into oncoming traffic. The truck hit them head on and they both died instantly. There were some things even being a werewolf couldn't save you from. They never got to see their granddaughter being born.

His parents left him their house, which was debt free, so Sarah and Zack moved out of their apartment and into the home he'd grown up in. Zack would never have gotten through those pain-filled weeks and months if not for Sarah. She gave birth to their beautiful baby girl the following March and they named her Hayley after his mum.

Valerie and Howard Stewart, Sarah's parents, didn't want anything to do with Hayley or Sarah as long as he remained in the picture. Zack and Sarah lived happily for nearly eighteen months before Sarah's disease really took hold. Then life was a constant juggle between work, day care for Hayley and hospital visits for Sarah. Sarah passed away peacefully in her sleep less than a month before Hayley's second birthday.

Two months after Sarah's passing, Zack received a surprise visit from the Department of Children's Services. They'd received an anonymous tip stating his daughter was in danger and naming Zack as an unfit parent. Zack knew who the tip had come from even if the social workers wouldn't reveal the name. He'd clung to Hayley while they searched his house from top to bottom before being forced to hand her over so they could perform an examination.

After they determined Hayley looked to be in good health and a happy two year old, they handed her back to Zack and left, letting him know they would be in contact.

Zack waited until Hayley was in bed that night before he picked up the phone and dialled a number he never thought he would. The line picked up on the fifth ring and Valerie's uppity, I'm better than you, voice rang through. "Hello, Valerie speaking."

"How dare you!" Zack was so furious that these people, who'd yet to even lay eyes on their granddaughter, said he was an unfit father.

"Excuse me? Who is this?"

"I said how dare you. What gives you the right to call Child Services and say I'm an unfit parent? You've never even met Hayley. You want nothing to do with her."

"Ah… Zack." Valerie's tone was really starting to get to Zack. "Yes, well, we can't have our only grandchild being raised by someone like you."

"Someone like me? What? You mean gay?" Zack was pacing his bedroom by this time with the phone clenched so tightly in his hand his knuckles were going white.

"Yes, that is exactly what I mean. You are an abomination and unless you repent, you will be going straight to hell along with Sarah."

Zack paused in stunned silence for a second. How could anyone think Sarah would go to hell? Furious at the people who were supposed to love her no matter what, Zack gritted his teeth and forced out, "You stay the hell away from me and my daughter." He hung up the phone and threw it at the wall.

Collapsing on his bed and curling into a ball, his body shook with the force of his crying. Zack had lost his parents, then his best friend, now these people were trying to take his daughter as well. He knew one thing though, he would fight them every step of the way. Hayley was his, and he would protect her with everything he had.

That's how Zack ended up on this lonely stretch of road, driving towards a town he'd never been before and starting a new job in a week's time. His only possessions were what he could fit inside his small Toyota Camry. Valerie and Howard came through on their threat and Zack was forced to sell his parents' house to afford the lawyers who fought his case in court.

Luckily the case hadn't dragged on for long. The judge was smart enough to see what the Stewarts were trying to do and, with the Department of Children's Services on his side, the judge awarded him sole custody of his daughter. Valerie and Howard were furious and vowed to get their only grandchild away from her perverted father.

After that, Zack thought it a good idea to move. There wasn't anything tying him to his hometown in the Blue Mountains. His parents and best friend were gone and the house he grew up in no longer belonged to him. He thought it best to get as far away from Sarah's parents as he could.

Zack searched online and found a teaching position available due to the current teacher being out on maternity leave. Zack applied for the position through the internet, then interviewed over the phone with the principal. Apparently a relief teacher had been taking the high school math classes for the last several weeks as they'd been unable to fill the position permanently. However, math was not her strong suit and the kids were being disadvantaged by this. No one wanted to move to a small town in the middle of nowhere anymore. For Zack, that was exactly what he wanted to do.

Zack received the phone call the following week letting him know he was the successful applicant for the position. He wasn't sure if they even received any other applicants but he wasn't about to argue. He thanked Donald Murphy, the principal, and said he could start at the beginning of the new school semester. School was currently out for midyear break but would be starting again the week after next.

Zack could barely contain his excitement about his new job. He loved teaching and missed not having a class to call his own when he cut his hours back when Sarah got sick. Zack looked forward to getting back into the classroom, but he didn't fool himself the kids would be excited to see him. They were teenagers and had much better things to do with their time. He didn't care. Zack loved the feeling he got when he saw understanding dawn on a teenager's face as the youth started to understand what he was trying to teach them.

One of the first things Zack did when he received the news he'd gotten the job was to call his Alpha and find out if there was a pack in the area. Jeremy Stretton was a good Alpha and looked after all his pack. He didn't discriminate over the colour of your skin or sexual preference. Alpha Stretton let him know a pack existed in the area and was led by a man named Alexander Holland. Alpha Stretton hadn't known much about the other Alpha as he'd only recently taken over the pack from his father and Stretton had only met the man once at the yearly Alpha gathering.

Alpha Stretton gave him the number he had on record for Alex Holland. Once Zack hung up with his Alpha, he called Alpha Holland and arranged to meet when he got to town. Zack was a little nervous, if truth be told, about meeting his new Alpha. He hoped he wasn't some bigoted asshole. He needed this job and didn't want to be forced to leave town before he even got to start work.

Zack had no idea how long he'd been lost in his thoughts but it must have been for some time as he noticed the welcome sign on the side of the road and realised he'd finally reached his new home.

Glancing in his mirror again, he saw Hayley still slept soundly and hoped she would stay that way long enough for Zack to find the hotel and check in. He slowed the car in accordance with the speed signs and the directions he printed from his computer showing the way to the hotel.

Navigating through the streets, Zack eagerly surveyed his surroundings and liked the look of the town. It was smaller than where he grew up in the mountains but he thought he could be happy here. Arriving at the hotel, he pulled up in the driveway and stopped in front of the reception. Zack left the car running in the hope Hayley would sleep for a little longer. He stretched out his muscles that threatened to cramp from sitting in a car all day. Once he felt a little better, he headed inside to check in.

A middle aged lady with slightly greying hair sat behind the counter and smiled at him as he approached.

"Good afternoon, Sir. How may I help?"

"Hi, I have a reservation for a week under the name Zack Bennett." Zack watched as the lady clicked away on the computer.

"Ah, yes. Here we are, a double bed with a port-a-cot." She read from the screen.

"Yes, thank you, if it's not too much trouble."

"Not at all, sir. The room should already be set up for you. If you just wait one moment, I'll get the paperwork." Zack nodded as she walked to the printer and waited for it to spit out the forms.

Zack stepped back and looked out the glass doors to the car, heaving a sigh of relief when he realised Hayley was still sleeping peacefully in her seat. Turning his attention back to the reception desk, he found the paperwork, with a pen, waiting for him to complete. After filling out the form and handing over his licence and credit card, Zack received his room key and a map of the hotel grounds which had his room circled with red ink.

"If you need anything else or there is something wrong with the room, please don't hesitate to call reception. Our hours are from seven am to eight pm."

"Thank you, I will." Zack picked up everything and headed back to his car. He drove around the side and found his room. After parking in the space provided, he once again left the car running until he had the room unlocked.

Opening the door to his current home, Zack looked around. The room wasn't much. For the money he was paying, he definitely wasn't expecting the plaza. The queen size bed dominated the room, with a brightly coloured quilt that looked faded from being washed so often.

After unbuckling Hayley from her car seat, Zack carried his daughter inside the room and gently laid her down in the port-a-cot. The cot barely fit between the left wall and his bed. Once he was sure Hayley was okay, Zack turned on one of the bedside lamps to give him a little light.

The carpet was an ungodly green colour; it looked to be stained in several places and worn in several others. It wasn't home by any means but it would do for a week or so while he looked for a place for him and Hayley.

Zack headed back to the car and started to unload his luggage. Placing his suitcases on the luggage rack and the small table, the room quickly filled with their belongings. On his third trip back to the car he heard his daughter cry out. Zack rushed back into the room and bent down over the cot to pick Hayley up. "Hey now, Pumpkin. Everything's okay," Zack reassured in his most soothing voice. He straightened himself up and patted her back as he rocked her a little.

Hayley's sniffles came to an end quickly and she leaned back to look him in the eyes. "Daddy, we stopped. Park now?"

Zack chuckled. "Yes, Hayley, we're here. Let me finish unloading the car then we can have a snack and go to the park." Zack kissed his beautiful little girl on the cheek and placed her back in the cot.

Hayley's excited screams about the park followed Zack as he went to get another load of boxes from the car. Half a dozen trips later, the car was finally empty. Zack went to the cooler he'd packed some food into with ice that morning and pulled out a yoghurt then found a spoon. Setting Hayley in one of the chairs at the table, Zack fed her the snack. When she was finished, Zack went to the bathroom and wet one of the face cloths and cleaned his daughter up. No matter what Zack tried, Hayley always seemed to end up with food all over her face. The mess was always worse when she fed herself.

Checking his watch, he noticed it was five to four. He'd arranged to meet with Alpha Holland at his place at five thirty. That gave him plenty of time to take Hayley to the park. He picked up the phone and dialled reception. After several rings the same lady who'd checked him in earlier answered. "Reception, how can I help you?"

"Hi this is Zack Bennett from room 122. I was wondering if there was a kids' play park nearby?"

"Yes, sir. If you head back to the main street and turn right, there's one not too far down on the left."

"Thank you, have a good day."

"You too, sir. Enjoy." Zack hung up the phone and made his way to Hayley.

"You ready to go play in the park, Pumpkin?"

"Yay!" Zack broke into a smile at his daughter's excitement. If only *his* life was that simple. Zack picked Hayley up and made his way out of the room and to his car while listening to the excited chatter of his two year old the entire way.

CHAPTER 2

"Do you have to do that here?" Simon didn't know exactly who he was talking to. All he wanted to do was relax after a long day at work, and he came home to find both his brothers and their mates making out in the living room. The television blared in the background, long since forgotten. Simon didn't begrudge his brothers their mates, it just seemed every time he turned around they were attempting to get into each other's pants. They could barely be in the same room together without constantly touching and, quite frankly, Simon was a little jealous.

Simon wanted to find someone who lit up the room when they walked in, someone whose touch caused his body to ache in such a good way, someone who looked at him as if he was their whole world, someone he could lose himself in and forget the world around him.

The growl coming from his brother, Alex, was actually quite impressive since he continued to kiss his mate, Jason, the entire time. Jason finally broke the kiss and giggled. He leaned his head back on the couch and looked up at Simon standing in the doorway. "Sorry."

Alex growled again. "Don't apologise, sweetheart. If he doesn't like it, he can always leave." Alex then started trailing kisses down Jason's neck.

Jason swatted Alex on the arm. "Be nice."

"Don't worry about it, Jase. I think I might go for a run. Give you all time to finish whatever you're doing here. Be back in about an hour." Simon turned and walked down the passage to his room. Running had always been one of his favourite things to do, whether in wolf or human form. Simon could always manage to lose himself and forget everything going on in his life in the rhythm of his feet hitting the ground.

In his room, Simon undressed and found his running clothes. Once dressed in shorts and a tank top, Simon slipped on his Nike running shoes and found his armband for his iPod before finding the device itself. Searching through his bedside drawers Simon then found his headphones. Connecting everything up and strapping the player in, Simon did some quick stretches then headed out of the house.

Simon jogged down the drive and turned left along the footpath. His body soon loosened up and he settled into a rhythm, heart beating steadily, feet pounding the pavement in time with the heavy base beat of the music. Simon cleared his mind and let all his thoughts and worries flow right out of him. All that mattered was putting one foot in front of the other, everything else could wait.

The sweat was soon dripping down his back and his leg muscles started to ache but Simon was just getting started. He turned down the main street of town, most of the shops already locked up this late in the afternoon on a Thursday. The footpaths were clear except for the occasional teenager on a bike. He passed the park where parents played with young children, gradually fading into older kids on skateboards and rollerblades as he neared the skate park.

Simon had resigned himself to never having kids. He'd suspected as young as fifteen he was gay. Kissing his best friend Mark after school when he was sixteen confirmed his suspicions. They'd fooled around together and he discovered what it was like to have sex with another boy.

He'd never been interested in girls. Simon knew who he was attracted to and didn't need to try anything with a girl to confirm his orientation. After all, why should he 'make sure' he didn't like girls, if straight guys didn't have to 'make sure' with another man? The whole thing seemed like a double standard to him.

Simon soon found himself at his turning point and he crossed to the other side of the street and headed back the way he'd come. A half hour later Simon's hair was wet with sweat as it dripped from his face and ran in rivulets down his back, his tank top plastered to his skin, and his leg muscles burning. Simon finally turned onto his street and noticed a Toyota Camry parked out front of his house. He didn't recognise the car and it had out of state plates. Must be the new pack member Alex had told him about.

Simon stopped on the front lawn and took ten minutes to do cool-down stretches. If he didn't, his body would rebel against him. His muscles would cramp and he would barely be able to walk.

Once Simon finished his stretches, he turned his iPod off and pulled his shirt off over his head. Simon hated the feeling of his sweat soaked clothes clinging to his body when he finished exercising. Making his way to the house, Simon pushed open the front door and stopped at the sight before him.

A little girl with bright red curls and the greenest eyes he'd ever seen stood in the passageway clutching a little wolf plush toy to her chest. Simon didn't want to frighten the small child so he quietly closed the door then crouched down with his back against the front door. "Hello there, pretty girl. What's your name?"

Simon watched as the girl's eyes roamed over him.

"Hayley," came the soft sweet reply.

"Hello, Hayley. I'm Simon. How old are you?" Hayley seemed to think about it for a minute then held up the arm currently not holding her toy, displaying two fingers.

"Two, oh wow! You're almost a big girl." Hayley's smile broke across her face and she nodded her head in agreement. "And who is this?" Simon asked, pointing to the stuffed wolf in her arms

"Woofie." Hayley thrust her toy out in front of her so Simon could get a good look. Her voice held certainty, she knew exactly who her teddy was. Simon smiled at her and patted the toy wolf.

"Hayley?" The most beautiful voice Simon had ever heard made its way to his brain. Hayley turned her head and squealed in delight as the voice was quickly followed by the most stunning man Simon had ever seen.

Roughly five foot nine with pale skin, freckles dusting his nose, the plumpest pink lips and a shock of red hair that was just long enough to run his fingers through, stood a man who took his breath away. With hair that colour, he would surely have to be this little girl's father. Right? Simon's thoughts were confirmed as the girl ran up and jumped at the man crying out, "Daddy."

Simon heard an 'Umph' as the man caught the young girl. Simon ran his gaze down the stranger's body and came to a halt at his crotch when he noticed a rather impressive bulge behind the jeans' zipper. He sucked in a breath at the sight before his eyes, that's when the scent hit him. It was like being hit between the eyes with a hammer. All his relaxed muscles tensed and his cock, which was already half hard at the sight of the man and his impressive package, hardened completely, draining the rest of the blood from his body and pooling it in his tight running shorts.

The scent was tickling his senses. It smelled like warm summer rain and something else Simon thought might be baby powder but wasn't sure. He couldn't believe it. His mate was in his house… and he had a child.

Simon put his hand on his knees and kept his back against the door as he slowly pushed himself up. He didn't want to scare his mate. He noticed the man's eyes work their way down his body then quickly lift back up when they got as far as his groin. The pink blush that stained his cheeks was sexy as hell and all Simon could think about at that moment was kissing this gorgeous man.

Simon took one step forward before Alex's voice broke through his fog. "Zack, did you find her? Is everything alright?" His brother's larger frame followed his voice from around the corner and he was soon standing behind Zack. "Hey Simon, glad you're home. Good run?"

"What?" Simon shook his head trying to remember what he was doing. Right, run. He had been running. "Ah, yeah, it was okay."

"This is Zack Bennet. He's just moved here from the Blue Mountains. And this little cutie is his daughter, Hayley." Alex grinned as he lightly tickled Hayley. She squealed and squirmed in her father's arms.

Simon nodded and stepped forward again and held out his hand. "Nice to finally meet you." Zack's blush seemed to darken as he reached out and shook Simon's hand.

"You too," was the softly spoken reply. Electricity race through Simon's hand and up his arm, all from one small touch. He couldn't wait to see what would happen if he ever got the chance to get his mate naked.

His thoughts about his naked mate were interrupted by his brother's deep voice. "Zack, would you and Hayley like to stay for dinner? It would be a good opportunity to get to know you a little better."

"Umm, okay, if you're sure it's no trouble." Zack stammered without taking his eyes off Simon's body.

Simon's cock grew impossibly harder in his running shorts and he felt sure his predicament was quite obvious.

"None whatsoever. Brian cooked up a huge pot of spaghetti Bolognaise so there's plenty of food."

Hayley screamed her enjoyment at hearing what was for dinner. "Yay, basketti bollolaise! Daddy, can I have some? I'm hungry." Simon smiled at the girl's pronouncement of their dinner and watched as she turned imploring eyes up to her father.

Zack seemed to shake himself and finally looked at his daughter. "You can have some when dinner is ready, Pumpkin." Then leaned in and kissed her lightly on the cheek before lowering her once again to the ground.

"How long until dinner, Alex? Do I have enough time to go shower?" Simon caught the sudden flair of heat in Zack's eyes at the mention of him showering.

"Yeah, you've got plenty of time."

With that Simon turned and headed towards his room. If he stayed any longer with Zack looking at him like that, he would jump the man right then and there, no matter who else was in the room.

Closing his bedroom door behind him, he quickly stripped out of the rest of his sweat-soaked clothes and made his way to the bathroom. Turning on the shower,

Simon let the water heat before stepping inside and rinsing the sweat and salt from his body.

Simon ached; he was hard enough to pound nails and what we really wanted was to go grab his mate and drag him into the shower with him. He knew that wasn't going to happen anytime soon, so he reached for the conditioner and poured a generous amount into his hand. Reaching down between his legs, Simon grasped his hard length and stroked from the base right to the tip, stopping to rub his finger through his slit. He groaned at the number of feelings shooting through his body with just that simple touch.

Simon let his imagination run wild as he thought about what it would be like if Zack joined him in the shower, kissing his mate until neither of them could breathe. He set a nice steady rhythm as he imagined himself kissing his way down Zack's neck, stopping every once in a while to lick at the water that ran in little rivulets down his mate's body. Simon would stop when he reached one of Zack's nipples and drive the man wild as he licked, sucked, bit and kissed the little nub before moving on to the other.

Simon's hand sped up, while his other reached down to cup and play with his balls. He could almost hear the moan coming from Zack's mouth before he would pull away from Simon and sink to his knees in front of Simon's hard, straining length.

Zack would lean in and run his tongue around his balls before sucking one, then the other, into his mouth, releasing each with a loud pop. Simon could almost feel his tongue on his shaft as he made his way up to the head and dipped his tongue into the slit to lap at all the pre-cum before opening his mouth and swallowing Simon down to the root.

Simon howled Zack's name as ropes of pearly white cum shot from his cock onto the tiles below to be washed away with the hot water. Leaning his arm against the wall, Simon took deep breaths trying to get his body to calm back down after the most explosive orgasm of his life. Once he was sure he could stand unaided, without the threat of his knees giving way, he washed the rest of his body and turned the shower off.

Quickly running a towel over his wet body, Simon walked to his closet. He wanted to get dressed and get back out to his mate as soon as possible. Grabbing a pair of well worn jeans he knew his ass looked great in, Simon found a shirt and pulled them both on, not bothering with underwear. He was already hard again at the thought of his mate and didn't want the extra layer of fabric constricting his body. Running his fingers through his hair, Simon was as ready as he would ever be.

* * * *

Zack sat at the dining room table surrounded by his mate's family. *His Mate*. Being gay, Zack never thought he would have a mate. Never thought there would be the perfect match for him out there. After everything he'd been through recently, he wasn't sure he could handle the fact he *did* indeed have a mate. Having nearly everyone he loved taken away from him, could he survive if he mated with Simon and then something happened to him as well?

Looking at his daughter sitting quietly in the chair next to him, Zack had another thought. What did Simon think about kids? Did he like them? Did he want one? Would he help Zack to raise Hayley? God this was such a mess.

"So Zack, what brings you to our small town?" Alex asked him. Their meeting earlier had been cut short when Zack realised Hayley wandered off, then with the invitation for dinner they never got back to it. It seemed Alex was going to continue the questions with the rest of the family present now.

"I got a job at the local High School while the current teacher is out on maternity leave. I'll be teaching math and social studies." Zack stopped and took a breath. His body stilled as the most glorious scent permeated his senses. The smell was rich, musky and all man with a hint of soap. Zack turned in his seat to see the drop dead gorgeous figure of his mate standing in the doorway. Simon had his arms crossed over his chest and his hip resting against the door jamb.

With his mate looking right at him, Zack smiled shyly and couldn't help but notice how sexy Simon looked in his faded jeans and tight black t-shirt, his hair still wet from his shower. A smile broke out across Simon's face as he pushed off the door jamb and stalked towards Zack. Zack's breath caught in his throat at the predatory look in Simon's eye.

Everything else faded into the background when Simon stopped in front of him. Simon raised a hand and cupped Zack's cheek and tingles started under his skin from the contact with his mate, making their way through his body straight to his cock. Simon's thumb brushed gently across his bottom lip before the hand cupping his cheek tipped his head backwards.

Zack's focus narrowed down to the lips in front of him, when Simon seductively leaned in for a kiss. Nothing else mattered at the moment except what it would feel like to have those lips pressed against his. He watched as a pink tongue darted out and licked the lips he so desperately wanted to taste before Simon finally closed the small distance still remaining between them.

A moan escaped from his throat as soft lips finally met his. The kiss was gentle and searching, not hard and demanding like he was expecting. Either way was fine by him. Zack opened his mouth when he felt Simon's tongue gently swipe against his bottom lip, right where his thumb had caressed earlier.

Simon's tongue invaded his mouth as the kiss deepened. The sound of a throat clearing cut through the fog created by the kiss; Simon broke away and rested his head against Zack's. They were both breathing fairly heavily; Simon kissed his lips once more before straightening and looking at the other people surrounding the table.

Zack could feel the heat rush to his cheeks at the realisation he had just shared his first kiss with his mate in front of Simon's entire family. Zack's heartbeat quickened at the thought his daughter had witnessed his kiss; he quickly turned to see her reaction only to find his daughter looking at him with a huge grin on her face.

"Daddy kissed a man." Hayley sang then broke into giggles. Everyone else at the table laughed at the stunned look on his face.

Simon pulled out the chair on the other side of Zack and took a seat at the table. Another throat cleared and Zack glanced up to see Alex staring at Simon with one eyebrow raised. "Umm Simon, is there something you want to tell me?"

Zack's mate leaned back in his chair with hands linked behind his head and sporting a cocky grin. "Nope."

The small chuckle from across the table pulled Zack's attention away from his mate and had him looking instead at Jason, Alex's mate. Jason winked at him and his smile lit up his face.

"Simon!" The name was practically a growl from the big Alpha.

Simon's grin never faded. "It's not like you haven't already guessed."

"I want to hear you say it."

"Fine then, Zack is my mate. Happy now?"

"Yep."

"It's yes not yep. Right, Daddy?" Hayley asked so

innocently Zack was hard pressed not to burst into laughter. Alex turned towards the little girl with an expression of complete and utter shock. Zack doubted anyone had ever dared correct the Alpha's speech before.

"Yes, Pumpkin, that's right."

Alex's attention was diverted away from Hayley and focused on Zack with his response and Zack swallowed the lump in his throat before straightening his shoulders and looking the man in the eyes.

"You got anything to add?"

"No." What more was there? Simon was his mate. They had a lot of things to talk about, but now wasn't the time.

"Well then, I suppose, welcome to the family. Mum will love you as you're going to make her dream of being a grandmother come true."

Before Zack could reply Brian arrived with dinner.

CHAPTER 3

Dinner was, once again, a noisy affair. Simon was used to this. Things had been very quiet for a while after Jason's attack in their home. Alex had replaced the dining room table since Jason couldn't stand to look at it. Simon couldn't blame him; being unable to move while a mad man tried to rape him a second time was bound to leave some scars.

With their family growing, the table had been getting a little small for them anyway so Alex bought a large one that could be extended when needed. It took several months but Jason was starting to get back to normal. Simon was sure there were still times when the nightmares gripped him but, thankfully, they seemed to be few and far between these days.

Looking over at Zack, Simon wasn't sure he would have had the strength not to kill the guy if something like that happened to his mate. He and Zack hadn't even completed their mating yet, but Simon could already feel his possessiveness towards Zack.

Biting back a growl, Simon concentrated on the conversation flowing around him. Everyone talked about their day and made plans for the coming weeks. They discussed pack business and set a time for their next dinner with their parents.

Simon was glad he had a close family, not like most households in this day and age. With parents getting divorced left, right, and centre, kids being dragged through custody battles, not to mention the parents that disowned their kids for being who they were. Brian and Jason had both experienced this after their parents found out they were gay. Simon was glad he was a werewolf as divorce was one thing he never had to worry about.

There wasn't a single case of destined mates splitting prior to death. He just hoped he and Zack could be as happy as his brothers were in their matings. Simon was a little nervous about Hayley. He had never thought a lot about kids since he knew from a young age he was gay and so assumed he would never have the opportunity to have any.

The little girl was cute as hell. With her green eyes and red curly hair, he knew Alex was right and their mother was going to go gaga over Hayley. That little girl was about to be spoiled rotten.

When all current topics seemed to be exhausted, Alex turned his attention back to Zack. "So Zack, you said you were a teacher. What made you decide you wanted to apply for this job in the first place? Did you have problems with your old pack?"

Simon turned to watch his mate. Zack seemed to take his time deciding what to say. The table sat in silence as everyone waited for an answer. "Never had any problems with my old pack."

"Did they know you were gay?" Brian interrupted

"Yeah, I came out when I was younger. My parents were great and the other members of the pack didn't care. I was never treated any differently." Zack smiled

"You were lucky," Jason commented. "Both Brian's and my parents and our birth pack turned their backs on us."

"Jeremy Stretton and his father William are great Alphas. There's never been any type of discrimination within the Blue Mountain Pack. As for why I decided to leave. There was nothing holding me there anymore but memories, and I needed to put some distance between my daughter and my hateful in-laws."

Simon was curious about his last statement. In-laws? Had Zack been married before? Was this person Hayley's mother or someone else? Zack had said he was gay so had he been married to a man or woman? God, Simon had so many questions, however he was beaten to the punch by Alex once again. "What do you mean hateful in-laws? If there is going to be problems, I need to know."

Simon looked over at Zack who had been wiping Hayley's face and hands clean of spaghetti sauce. Nodding once at Alex, he finished cleaning his daughter then picked her up and sat her on his lap. Cuddling Hayley close, Zack started to talk.

"My parents were killed in a head-on collision nearly three years ago." Simon inhaled sharply at the thought of his mate losing his parents. He didn't know what he would do if he lost his folks. Reaching over, Simon took Zack's hand and gave it a gentle squeeze. Zack returned the gesture and smiled at him.

"At the time my best friend, Sarah, was pregnant with our daughter. Sarah had been diagnosed with cancer and wasn't given very long to live. She didn't want the treatment because she wanted a child; she asked me to be the father. I agreed. I would have done anything for her. Mum and Dad gave us the money we needed and she got pregnant. They died before Hayley was even born. They never got to meet their grandchild."

Simon raised his hand and wiped away the tear that was slowly running down his mate's cheek. His heart broke for his mate; he'd suffered so much loss in his life already.

Simon wanted to take him in his arms and kiss all the hurt away. But he couldn't do that yet.

"Sarah's parents were like your old pack, Jason and Brian. They were extremely religious and wanted Sarah to have nothing to do with me. She refused so they basically disowned her. They wanted nothing to do with Hayley since she was the daughter of a filthy pervert, an abomination in their words. That all changed when Sarah succumbed to her disease."

Simon was continually astounded at the cruelty of some people. Looking over at the little girl snuggled in her daddy's arms, he didn't know how anyone wouldn't want anything to do with her. She was so cute and innocent, had barely had a chance to start a life.

"Not long after I'd buried the only other person in my life that I loved, apart from Hayley, they called child services on me. Said I was an unfit parent. I woke one morning to find two support workers on my doorstep. Apart from burying the people I loved, that was the worst experience of my life. I stood there and held Hayley as these strangers searched my house for evidence of my neglect."

Simon couldn't take it anymore. He moved his chair as close as he could and wrapped his arms around Zack, pulling him close. Zack sighed and leant back, resting his head against Simon's shoulder, before lightly kissing his neck. Zack then kissed Hayley on the head and finished his story.

"When nothing came of the house visit, the Stewarts got lawyers involved and took me to court for custody of Hayley. It seemed as long as their daughter was alive, they were fine with ignoring our existence, but once Sarah died they couldn't handle the idea of their only grandchild being raised by me."

Simon looked at the expressions on the faces of the rest of his family. Every single person at the table had similar looks of anger and disgust at the lack of tolerance of some people. He knew his face mirrored those of everyone else. Simon couldn't believe what Zack had endured in the last couple of years. How could someone think Zack would neglect his daughter? Simon had only known him for several hours and he could already tell how much his mate loved his daughter. That girl would never want for anything if it was within Zack's power to give her.

Tightening his hold on Zack, Simon listened as he finished his tale. "I was lucky to get a good judge who could see what the Stewarts were trying to do. Once the social workers got on the stand and said they couldn't find any evidence of neglect on my part and Hayley was a healthy, happy two year old, the judge had heard enough."

"I was awarded sole custody. Valerie and Howard weren't happy with the judge's decision and tried to appeal. The appeal was denied. The Stewarts vowed to get Hayley away from me no matter what any judge said. By this time, with the funeral costs and all the lawyers, I was out of money. I had to sell the house I'd grown up in; my parents had left it to me. With all the bad memories from the last eighteen months, I couldn't stay there any longer. Plus with the threat of Valerie and Howard, I couldn't risk anything happening to Hayley. I had nothing left holding me in town so I packed all our possessions, found a new job and here I am."

Zack seemed to hold his breath when he finished talking, waiting to see what the reaction to his story would be. His answer wasn't long in coming.

"Holy Shit!" Jason exclaimed

"Those bastards." Rick joined in.

Alex sat there stony-faced for a minute before he finally spoke. "Do you think the Stewarts were serious in their threat to take Hayley from you?"

Zack seemed to think about his answer. "Yeah, I do. After everything they've put me through, I don't think they're just going to let this drop."

"It's okay, you're not alone anymore." Simon tried to reassure his mate.

Zack bit his bottom lip before slowly nodding his head. "I'm really sorry to bring this problem to your doorstep. I wish they would just leave me alone. I've never done anything to them. They even liked me before they found out I was gay."

Alex shook his head "Don't worry about it. You're family now, even if you haven't completed the mating yet. Even if you weren't, we would help you; we're not in the habit of turning those away that are in need of help. Plus when mum finds out you've made her a grandmother, you're going to come face to face with one protective woman."

Jason and Brian giggled at Alex's description of his mother. Hayley looked up from where she'd been cuddling her daddy at the sound of the laughter. Glancing around the table her gaze settled on Simon. A wide grin spread across her face before she quickly turned and launched herself from her father's arms straight at Simon.

Simon grunted as he caught the flying two year old before he pulled her in close for a cuddle.

"Hayley, please be gentle." Zack admonished his

daughter.

"It's okay, she didn't hurt me. More surprised me than anything." Simon turned his attention to the grinning redhead in his arms. "Well, hello there, darlin'. Did you enjoy your dinner?" Simon smiled at the quickly bobbing head. "Would you like some ice cream for dessert? Maybe with some chocolate topping?"

The gigantic smile coming from that small face, with her chubby checks still lightly stained with spaghetti sauce caused Simon's heart to skip a beat. Simon knew in that moment he would do everything possible to keep this young girl, who would one day be as much his daughter as Zack's, safe. Simon leant down and lightly kissed Hayley on her cheek. "Hmm spaghetti, yummy."

Hayley giggled, and then her eyes lit up as Brian placed a bowl with vanilla ice cream with chocolate topping on the table in front of her. "Thank you," sang the delicate voice from the little girl in his lap before she picked up her spoon and started eating. Simon kept hold of her while she messily ate her dessert. Looking over at Zack, Simon wasn't sure what the look on his face meant but it gave him hope for the future he wanted with these two wonderful people.

* * * *

Zack watched his daughter sitting in his mate's lap eating ice cream and loved the sight before him. He couldn't believe how quickly Hayley took to Simon, although he shouldn't be surprised. Hayley never had any trouble getting to know new people and was always looking for cuddles no matter where they came from. She always managed to wrap any adult around her little finger within minutes of meeting.

Zack could feel eyes on him and glanced up to see Simon watching him. Simon seemed happy; Zack leant forward and brushed a kiss across his lips. Not wanting to take things further with Hayley on Simon's lap, Zack settled back in his chair.

The conversation around the dinner table turned to everyone's plans for the upcoming weekend. Zack sat quietly and listened. His plans for the weekend included trying to find a place for Hayley and him to live. He'd paid for a week at the hotel and really hoped he wouldn't have to extend the stay longer than that. As much as he loved his daughter, he wanted a room to himself again. Sharing a space with Hayley severely limited what he could do once she was asleep for the night.

Turning his gaze towards his mate again had all sorts of thoughts racing through his mind, thoughts of things they could get up to if they had some privacy. Zack could just imagine the hard chiselled body of the sexy as hell man in front of him; could imagine running his tongue around dark brown nipples before sucking one into his mouth and biting down gently. Zack could almost feel Simon's naked body pressed against his own as Simon gradually slid his hard thick cock deep within his aching body.

Zack's cock, which had hardened at some point during his runaway thoughts, released a small bead of pre-cum. Shit! Shaking his head to try and clear his lusty thoughts, Zack couldn't believe he'd gotten hard thinking about his mate in front of Simon's entire family and his daughter. Zack's cheeks burned as the blood ran to his face.

Realizing he had closed his eyes while fantasising, he reluctantly opened them to find everyone at the table staring at him and trying to hold back their laughter.

Jason sat forward and patted his hand, his face still lit up like he was holding back a laugh. "Don't stress about it. We've all been there. Hell, I was showing off my new nipple piercings to Brian when Maryanne and Joe walked in. Talk about embarrassing." Zack chuckled at Jason's story.

Simon leant forward and whispered in his ear. "I don't know what thoughts were going though that pretty head of yours but I'm thinking I would love a live action replay at some point." Simon's tongue flicked out and licked the lobe of his ear before he pulled it into his mouth and nibbled on the sensitive flesh. Zack felt his cock throb again and his body shiver at the sensations Simon was causing to shoot through in his body.

Simon chuckled at his reaction before kissing the side of his neck and pulling away. "Can you stay for a little longer or do you need to get back to where you're staying?" Zack looked down at his watch and noticed it was getting on towards eight o'clock. He really needed to get going.

Looking into Simon's eyes, he hoped he was conveying how much he really wished he could stay. "I'm sorry, but it's getting late and it's past Hayley's bedtime. I really need to get her back and showered and put down for the night, otherwise, she's going to be really grumpy tomorrow. I wish I could stay."

Simon smiled at him before leaning in for another brief kiss. "I understand," Simon whispered against his lips. Pulling back, he turned Hayley around in his arms so she was facing him. "Now you, princess, be good for your daddy, okay?" Simon tickled her sides and gave her a kiss on the cheek as she squealed with laughter. Giving her a last quick hug, Simon then handed her back to Zack.

"Thank you for a wonderful evening. Dinner was delicious. I look forward to getting to spend some more time with you all." With that, Zack stood, Hayley in his arms.

Alex stood and extended his hand to shake. "It was our pleasure. You're welcome anytime you like. You're family after all. We'll organise to have you officially join the pack next week after you're settled in." Zack extended his hand and clasped it in the strong grip of his new Alpha. Letting go, Zack stood back and felt electricity shoot up his spine as Simon placed a hand at the middle of his back.

"I'll walk you out." Zack couldn't reply as all the saliva seemed to have disappeared from his mouth. God, this man's touch sent his body into overdrive. Nodding his assent, he turned and followed Simon through the passage and out the front door.

They walked together to Zack's car and Simon kissed Hayley again on the cheek before wishing her a good night. He waited as Zack unlocked the car and got Hayley settled in her seat and buckled in. Closing the door, Zack turned and found himself engulfed in the strong arms of his mate. "Hmm," Zack snuggled in against Simon's strong chest. He felt a soft tongue against his neck and moaned at the wonderful feeling. Lips followed the tongue before Simon slowly pulled away.

"Drive safe and think about me tonight." Simon's smile was addictive.

"No worries there. I'll be lucky if I can get you out of my thoughts tonight." Simon laughed at his confession. He stepped back and walked to the driver's side. Biting his lower lip for a minute, Zack asked the question that was burning in the back of his brain, dying to get out. "Can we see you tomorrow?" His cheeks heated at the desperate note in his voice.

The reply was quick in coming and calmed his nerves a little. "Absolutely. I'll be counting down the hours. Maybe we could all go out for dinner or something?"

"Sounds great." Zack knew the smile on his face was a mile wide as he got in his car and started it. Putting the car in gear, he looked out the window at his mate one last time before he pulled away from the house. He watched in his mirrors as he drove down the street. Simon stayed standing on the curb the entire time.

Zack drove back to the motel, his thoughts back at the house he'd just left. He groaned as his cock twitched in his pants, reminding him he was still hard and wanting with no relief in sight. Zack loved his daughter, but he really would have loved some alone time with Simon as well. Looking in the backseat, he noticed Hayley was happy sitting and chattering away to herself.

Pulling up outside his hotel room, Zack turned the car off and got out. He adjusted his hard cock so it wasn't quite so painful before getting Hayley and making his way into their room. "Okay, Pumpkin, shower then a story and bed. How does that sound?"

"Okay, can we read the ladybird book?"

"Sure, sweetheart. Get ready for your shower while I try and find it." The Ladybird book was Hayley's favourite story; she just about knew all the words and loved the pop-up illustrations. Zack had made a point to pack the book in his case so he would be able to get to it easily.

Once Hayley was washed, dried, and dressed in her favourite pink princess pyjamas, they cuddled up on the bed so Zack could read her the story. Halfway through, Zack heard a little snore and looked down. Smiling at the angelic look on his daughter's face, he moved her gently and placed her in her cot. She was getting to be too big for a cot, he would have to think about getting her a big girl bed when he found somewhere for them to live.

Zack made sure woofy was within easy reach and tucked her in tight. He then had a quick shower and crawled into bed wearing a pair of boxers. Zack usually preferred to sleep naked but with his daughter in the room decided a little modesty was in order. He was exhausted; he had started a new life today, in a new town with a new job and apparently a new mate. Zack hadn't expected to meet his mate but after spending a little time with Simon he couldn't be happier with who the fates had chosen for him. Now if only they could get some time alone together. With that thought Zack drifted into a peaceful sleep filled with images of Simon and himself curled together in bed.

CHAPTER 4

Simon hadn't been able to concentrate all day. Work passed slowly without any major drama, which was great as he wouldn't have been in the right frame of mind to deal with it anyway. As it was, the spreadsheets he worked on made no sense to him today and no matter how many times he tried, he couldn't get the damn things to balance. Simon was thankful he didn't have any meetings and that it was Friday.

He called Zack during lunch and just the sound of his mate's voice soothed his soul. They talked for his entire lunch break as Hayley had her afternoon nap. Zack was going to pick him up tonight since he had a seat in his car for Hayley and they would all go out for dinner.

As soon as five o'clock came round he was out of the office and headed home. He wanted to have a shower and get ready for his date. Could you really call it a date if you had a two year old with you? Shrugging his shoulders, Simon decided it was a date no matter who was with them. Hayley was a part of the package and it would be nice to spend time with the both of them.

Pulling into the driveway at home, Simon waited for the carport door to open, As he wasn't using his car tonight he may as well put the vehicle away and leave room for everyone else's cars. They might have to start thinking about expanding. With everyone finding their mates, they kept adding cars as well as people to the house. There were currently six different types of vehicles that were vying for parking space and if he could convince Zack to move in with them then he would add a seventh. Deciding to talk to his brothers about the space issue over the weekend, Simon locked his car and went inside.

He found Brian in the kitchen making a start on dinner. Walking to the fridge, he grabbed a beer and took a seat to chat with his brother-in-law for a few minutes.

"So are you going to be in for dinner?"

Simon could feel the smile breaking out across his face at the thought of going out with Zack. "Nah, man."

"Ohhh! Does someone have a date?"

Simon laughed at Brian's teasing tone. "Zack and Hayley will be by to pick me up; we're going out for dinner."

"That girl is so cute. You're so lucky, Simon." Simon frowned slightly at the wistful tone to Brian's voice now. He knew Brian and Marcus really wanted kids.

"Hey, man, none of that. You and Marcus are going to make great parents. It will happen for you. You just have to wait and see. I'm right." Simon downed the rest of his beer before walking over and giving Brian a gentle squeeze. "It'll happen when the time is right. I don't know how, but you two were meant to be parents. Same with Jason and Alex," and with that Simon headed to his room to start getting dressed.

Simon knew deep in his gut he was right, his brothers were meant to be parents. He didn't know if they would have to get a surrogate or if they were going to adopt, he just knew they would have the kids they always wanted. Getting undressed, Simon made his way into his bathroom.

After a quick shower and a shave, Simon grabbed his favourite pair of jeans and pulled them on; when he wasn't working he preferred to go commando. He loved the freedom and the feel of not being constricted. Plus he was already half hard and didn't want anything in the way if he should get at all lucky tonight. Simon did up his belt and pulled on a nice deep blue button up shirt. He'd been told he looked great in the shirt and wanted to look nice for Zack.

Simon sat on the edge of his bed and pulled on his black boots. Alex was the only one in the family who rode a motorcycle but all the brothers seemed to have similar fashion with the boots and leather jackets. He walked into the bathroom and checked his appearance in the mirror. "Not too bad, if I do say so myself." Simon chuckled to himself.

Being a werewolf, he forewent any cologne as the smell irritated his senses. Simon grabbed his jacket and headed into the living room. Everyone else was home from work and they were all relaxing, having a beer on a Friday afternoon. Simon snapped his head to the left when he heard a wolf whistle.

"Well, don't you look hot." Jason said grinning at him. Simon laughed as Alex growled and pulled Jason closer against his chest. "What? He does." Jason said as he smacked Alex's chest.

"You aren't supposed to be looking at my brothers." Alex's growl came out deep and grumbly.

"Oh don't be ridiculous. You know you're the only one for me." Jason said as he leant forward and placed a soft kiss against Alex's lips. Alex growled again and deepened the kiss. Simon just chuckled and took a seat. Alex was so possessive over Jason. Although after everything the little man had been through, he couldn't really blame his brother.

Simon gave the pair thirty seconds to quit what they

were doing before he picked up a cushion and threw it at them. Brian and Marcus laughed at the shocked expression on Alex's face. Simon would have laughed as well if the doorbell hadn't rung. His heartbeat accelerated at the thought of seeing his mate again. Getting up from his seat he headed to the door.

Opening the door he had just enough time to see a pink blur and hear his name being called in a sweet little girl voice before he was nearly knocked on his ass as a pair of little arms wrapped around his legs.

"Hayley, please be careful. You nearly knocked Simon over." Simon looked up into the beautiful face of his mate and smiled.

"Hi," Zack managed to get out before Simon reached out to him and threaded his fingers behind his neck and dragged him close. Their lips sealed together and Simon groaned at the first taste of his mate all day. The kiss was cut short however by an insistent tug on his jeans. Breaking away from Zack, Simon reached down and picked Hayley up in his arms.

"And hello to you too, Princess. Don't you look pretty in your pink dress!" Simon honestly hated pink. He thought there couldn't have been a worse colour ever invented, but looking at the girl in his arms who was swaying back and forth holding the skirt of her dress proudly, Simon had a bad feeling there would be a lot of pink in his life from now on.

Hayley beamed up at him. "Daddy said I look cute as a button. Do you like my piggy tails? Daddy did them. Are we going out? I'm hungry and Daddy said we were having dinner with you." Simon's head was reeling as the little girl spewed one question after another.

"Whoa there, sweetheart! One question at a time." Simon chuckled. "You look adorable, your hair is beautiful and yes, we are going out to dinner."

"Sorry," Zack said. "She's at that stage where she wants to know everything."

"No problem. I'm sure I'll get used to it in time. Now how about we head out so this little one can get something to eat." Simon said as he tickled Hayley in the belly. Her squeals of laughter were met with a smile from Zack. "Come in and we'll say goodnight to the guys."

Simon reached out and took Zack's hand while he moved Hayley to his hip. Turning around, Simon led them towards the full living room.

Simon watched as Zack greeted his brothers and their mates and settled into a comfortable conversation about their days. He wasn't really paying much attention to what was said until Rick's voice broke through his thoughts.

"You three look good together." Simon was surprised by the comment from Rick but couldn't help the smile that broke across his face. He looked at Zack and noticed the pink staining his cheeks. Simon squeezed Zack's hand before turning back to his family.

"Thanks, man. We're heading out so you guys have a good night."

After all the goodbyes, they went outside to Zack's car. Zack took Hayley and buckled her into her seat. Simon slid into the passenger seat and was surprised at how clean the car was. With a two year old and after a long road trip, Simon wasn't expecting the clean interior. The car couldn't have been more than a couple of years old.

Once Zack joined him and started the car, they pulled out of the driveway.

"So where to?" Zack asked.

"I was thinking about the steakhouse. I know it's not real romantic but they do a hell of a steak and I believe they have stuff to keep kids entertained." Simon wasn't sure what type of food Zack liked but he figured as he was a werewolf he would go with steak. It seemed pretty safe.

"Steak sounds fantastic. I've haven't had a decent

one in ages." Simon gave directions and within 10 minutes they were pulling into the car park of the local steakhouse. Zack and Simon got out of the car and Simon headed to the backseat to unclip Hayley. Once she was out of the car, Simon took one of her hands and Zack took her other one.

Walking into the restaurant they stopped at the counter to wait to be seated. It didn't take long before one of the waitresses came up to them.

"Hey Simon, what brings you out tonight without your brothers?" Isabella was pack and her parents owned the place so he wasn't at all surprised to see her working.

"Hey Bella, we're on a date. This is my mate, Zack, and his daughter Hayley."

"Mate… Oh wow… You must be so happy. I can't wait till I find my mate." Simon could see the genuine happiness she had for him on her face. "So table for three, then?" Bella went around the counter to consult her book before coming back with the menus and some crayons for Hayley. "Right this way."

Simon and Zack followed Bella through the restaurant until she stopped at a table and placed the menus down. Once they were seated, she set a couple of colouring pages and a cup of crayons down. "There you go, sweetheart."

"Thank you."

"Oh, what wonderful manners. Can I get you boys something to drink?" After taking their orders, Isabella walked away promising to return with their drinks. Looking around, Simon noticed the restaurant was about half full. It was still early and new; the place would pick up soon.

Five minutes later, they had their drinks and their orders placed. Simon reached across the table when Zack put his beer down and took his hand, running his thumb across the back of Zack's hand. Simon let his gaze wander around the restaurant and groaned when he realised who had just walked through the doors.

"What's wrong?" Zack asked with a puzzled expression on his face.

"I hope you don't mind but I believe you're about to meet my parents." Simon said as he watched his parents notice him and head in their direction, ignoring the table Isabella was trying to show them to.

"What?" Zack choked out.

"Yeah, sorry, was hoping to keep you to myself tonight but it doesn't seem to be working out that way." Simon turned away from his obviously nervous mate and gazed up at his parents. His dad was grinning from ear to ear and his mom had a perplexed expression on her face.

Simon stood when his parents arrived and gave his mum a kiss on the cheek. "Hey, mum, dad. What are you guys doing out for dinner?"

"Oh, your father's taking me out for our anniversary."

"Nice and romantic, Dad." His dad chuckled at him.

"Oh stop it. You know what he's like. Give him a steak and he's a happy man. This place is fine. It's just nice to go out." He watched as his mum's eyes kept darting back and forth between himself, Zack, and Hayley.

Simon looked at Zack and grinned. He didn't want to ruin the surprise too soon. He looked back at his parents in time to see his mum elbow his dad in the ribs. Chuckling, he looked at his dad and raised an eyebrow.

His dad sighed "So son, are you going to introduce us?" He knew his dad couldn't deny anything his mum wanted and what she wanted most of all, right now, was to know who he was with.

Looking at Zack, he couldn't help but grin as he made the introductions. "Zack, these are my parents, Maryanne and Joe Holland. Mum, Dad, this is my mate, Zack Bennett and his daughter, Hayley. His attention rushed back to his mum at her quickly indrawn breath. One hand was covering her mouth and the other seemed to be squeezing the life out of his dad's arm.

"Mr and Mrs Holland, it's lovely to meet you. Your sons are wonderful men." Zack held his hand out for his dad to shake.

His father shook his mate's hand and grinned widely. "It's nice to meet you too, young man. Welcome to the family. Please call me Joe."

Simon looked at Hayley who sat quietly watching everything. Simon held out his hand for her. "Hey Princess, can you come here for a minute? There's someone I would like you to meet." Hayley nodded as she stood and walked around the table before she took Simon's hand.

Simon looked at his mother and smiled at her. "Hayley, this is my mum and dad." Simon looked at Zack to make sure what he was doing was okay. The smile and nod he got in return, let him know his mate was happy for him to continue. "You can call them Nanna and Poppy if you like."

Hayley looked up and him and smiled, "Okay." She let go of Simon's hand before she walked up to his mother and looked up at her. "Hello. Do you like my dress?" Her soft melodic voice questioned before she lifted her arms in the universal symbol of 'Up.'

Simon watched his mother as a tear ran down her

cheek before she bent and picked the little girl up into her arms and crushed her in a hug. "Your dress is beautiful and so are you."

Simon looked away from the sight when he heard a throat clearing. Looking at his dad, he couldn't help but be in awe of the love he could see shining on his face for his wife. He hoped he and Zack would be that happy in the future.

"You do realise your mother is going to spoil that poor child rotten. And I'm never going to get a moment's peace around the house anymore." Simon just laughed and nodded.

"So Zack, Alex tells me you're a teacher."

"Yes, Sir. Math is my main subject but I also teach social studies."

"Alex told you about Zack?" That would probably explain the grin on his face when his dad had seen him sitting there with Zack.

"Yep, and let me tell you, keeping that a secret from your mother was one of the hardest things I've ever done. Thank god, we saw you tonight, I don't know if I could have kept something as big as a grandchild from her for very long."

Simon laughed again. His dad had never been able

to hide anything from his mum.

"Anyway, Zack, it was nice to meet you and I'm sure we'll get plenty of opportunities to get to know you better, but we should really head to our table and let you get back to your evening."

"You too, Joe, Maryanne, enjoy your dinner." Zack took Hayley's hand and led her back to the table. Not two minutes after they settled down again, their meals arrived. Simon watched as Zack took a bite of his steak, which was quickly followed by the most sexual noise he had ever heard.

Simon had to bite back his own growl as his cock hardened at the moans coming from his mate. "Enjoying that steak, are we?" Zack's eyes snapped open and a blush covered his cheeks. God, he was gorgeous.

"Sorry. Didn't realise I was doing that. This meat just melts in your mouth. And it's cooked to perfection."

Simon looked at Hayley who was happily dunking her own piece of steak and chips in tomato sauce before attempting to get them in her mouth. Leaning across the table, Simon lowered his voice so he was sure Hayley wouldn't hear him "It's fine, but next time I hear that noise coming from your mouth, I would prefer it if we were in bed and naked."

* * * *

Zack could feel his cheeks heat even further before he put his knife and fork down. The thought of him and Simon being naked in bed had his cock sitting up and waving hello. However, it wasn't as simple as that. He had Hayley to think about. He needed to make sure Simon was in this for the long haul. That the idea of helping him to raise Hayley for the rest of their lives was what he wanted.

Zack had been nervous about meeting Simon's parents. He definitely wasn't expecting it to happen in the middle of a restaurant on their very first date. Maryanne had loved Hayley and that was a good sign. She needed grandparents to spoil her. The thought that his parents never got the opportunity hurt his heart. It hurt even more knowing her other biological grandparents were cruel, bigoted assholes.

Zack shook his head trying to get his thoughts back to where they needed to be. Looking over the table at his mate, he noticed Simon had stopped eating as well and was watching him. He seemed to be waiting for whatever Zack was going to say.

Schooling his nerves, Zack bit the bullet. "As much as I would love to fulfil that idea, I need to know how you feel about Hayley first. You have to understand, this is a package deal. I'm all she has left and I won't give her up for anything. Not even my mate."

Zack was watching Simon closely and didn't miss the hurt that quickly flashed across his face before being replaced with something Zack hoped was understanding. "I would never ask you to give up Hayley. She is a part of you and will always be. As soon as I met you, I knew this was a package deal. I admit I'd never really thought about kids before, but I'm not against them and Hayley is a beautiful little girl."

Simon reached across the table and once again took his hand that had started to shake. Giving the hand a gentle squeeze he continued. "I've never really been around kids much, apart from my brothers so you're going to have to help me. I want us to be a family. I want my mate and, I hope one day, Hayley can be our daughter along with any other children that may come along."

Zack didn't know what to say. Actually he didn't know if he could say anything to that. The lump that had taken up residence in his throat felt like it was the size of a tennis ball. Instead he sat there and nodded his head as tears streaked down his face.

He watched as Simon stood up and walked around the side of the table until he crouched down bedside Zack's chair. The feel of Simon's hand gently cupping his cheek and wiping away his tears was so wonderful to his touch-starved body. The soft whisper of his mate's voice had shivers running down his spine. "We'll work it out as we go, honey. You're mine and I'm not letting either of you go." A soft kiss was placed on his lips before Simon stood and resumed his seat at the table.

"Daddy, are you okay? Why are you crying?" Hayley's voice broke through the fog that was trying to take hold. Turning to face his daughter, Zack couldn't help but let out a bark of laughter at the sight before him.

Hayley had managed to get sauce everywhere. And when he said everywhere, he meant it. The sauce was in her hair, on her dress, up her arms, on her forehead, and all over the table. The only place it seemed she didn't get the sauce was the napkin he had tucked in the front of her dress.

Zack could hear Simon chuckling across from him. "I'm fine, Pumpkin. Look at you though, you're a mess." Hayley just beamed up at him, like it was everyday she went around wearing tomato sauce. "It's all Simon's fault, isn't it, sweetie?" Zack laughed as he started to wipe his daughter down.

"Me? What did I do?" Zack could hear the mock

horror in Simon's voice as he tried to defend himself against the allegations.

"Yeah, it's all Simon's fault." Zack laughed and Hayley giggled along with him as they condemned their dinner companion.

"Fine, okay. I admit it was me. I was trying to make a tomato sauce monster. How do you think I did?"

"I think you succeeded." Zack admitted as he wiped the sauce from Hayley's hair. Once Hayley was semi-respectable again, he helped her finish her dinner as he and Simon finished theirs. They ordered Hayley some ice cream while they sat and sipped on coffee. Zack couldn't help but smile across the table at Simon. He didn't think he'd been this happy since the day his daughter was born, and even then that happiness wasn't complete as he could tell the toll everything had taken on Sarah's body.

"What are you thinking about?" Simon's question dragged his mind back to the here and now.

"Huh?"

"You looked really happy for a moment and then your expression fell like you were remembering something sad." Zack wasn't aware he showed his thoughts so clearly, but it wasn't anything he wanted to keep secret so he told Simon what he had been thinking about.

"Happy looks good on you." Zack could feel his lips turning up at the corners with that pronouncement.

"Yeah?"

"Yeah. I think I'm going to make it my mission in life that you're always to be happy and smiling." Simon lowered his voice a little "You look sexy as hell when you smile."

Zack couldn't help the blush that rose up his cheeks or the wide smile from forming on his face. The fact this beautiful, intelligent and sexy-as-sin man in front of him wanted to make him happy for the rest of his life caused his body to heat and his heart to melt.

"Come home with me tonight. Please?"

"Simon." Zack sighed. God, he wished he could. He wanted nothing more in that moment than to go back to Simon's and get naked and sweaty with his mate. Just thinking about it had his cock hardening against his pants. "I wish I could but I have Hayley."

"I know, Zack." Simon reached over and caressed his cheek. Zack couldn't help but turn into the touch. "I understand anything we do from here on out will include Hayley and I'm fine with that. I was suggesting we go back to the hotel and get what you will need for the night. There is a guest room right next door to mine at home."

Zack had to admit he really wanted to agree. Spending the night with his mate would be wonderful but having a two year old in the house could be a little distracting. For everyone. "What about everyone else, Simon? It's not like you live alone and having a two year old in the house can be exhausting."

"The guys will be fine with it. Marcus and Brian want kids anyway and, I think, Alex and Jason are going to want them soon as well. As for Rick, he's been going out a lot recently so he shouldn't have a problem with it either."

Zack bit his bottom lip. He was so tempted just to say yes but he needed to make sure Hayley would be happy with the situation. Looking at his daughter, he didn't care how difficult it made his life by having a two year old, he wouldn't change her for the world. "Hey, Pumpkin?"

"Yes, Daddy?" Hayley looked at him. She had finished her dessert and started back in on her colouring, sticky fingers and all.

"Would you like to sleep over at Simon's house tonight? You'll get to sleep in a big bed, but Daddy won't be in the same room. Just like it was before we moved here, I will be in the room next to yours."

Hayley looked like she really thought about what he had said. He wasn't sure how much of what he told her she really understood, considering her age but she looked cute anyway.

"Will I still get to sleep with Woofie?"

"Of course, we'll go and get your princess jammies and some clothes for tomorrow."

The grin that broke across his daughter's face at the mention of her favourite pyjamas was priceless. So was the excited bobbing of the head and the loud "Yay!"

"I take it that means yes?" Simon said, chuckling.

"It does indeed." Zack replied, turning to look at his mate. He knew all the heat and desire he felt for Simon was visible in his eyes. He couldn't wait to get his hands on his mate's naked body.

Zack watched as Simon discreetly reached below the table and adjusted himself. "I think it's time to pay the bill and get going, don't you?" Simon asked as he stood up and walked around the table to help Hayley pack up her colouring.

Yeah, it was definitely time to go. The sooner they left, the sooner they could get to the good stuff. Zack just hoped Hayley would sleep through the night.

CHAPTER 5

Simon couldn't believe how hard his cock was as they pulled up outside his house. Images of what his mate would look like naked and writhing under him had plagued him the whole way from the restaurant. His wolf was riding him to lay claim to his mate and Simon was just as impatient, but knew they needed to get Hayley settled for the night before either he or his wolf would get what they wanted.

Getting out of the car, Simon grabbed Zack's overnight bag while Zack released Hayley and pulled her out of the car. "Let's get this tomato sauce monster washed and in bed, huh?" Hayley giggled at him as he tickled her side lightly.

"Sounds like a plan," Simon agreed with him.

Simon held Zack's hand as they headed inside. It wasn't late and the others, less Rick, were all in the living room watching the Friday night football game. Simon wasn't sure what was wrong with his youngest brother but he was starting to worry a little. Recently, Rick had been going out nearly every night and not coming in till after everyone else was fast asleep.

He was spending his nights going from one bar to

another and Simon was getting worried. Werewolves couldn't get drunk, their bodies metabolised the alcohol too quickly. So what was Rick doing if he wasn't drinking himself into a stupor? It was something he should talk to Alex about. Maybe in the morning; he had other things to concentrate on tonight instead of what was going on with his brother.

Alex looked up at them as they walked into the room. "Evening." Alex caught sight of the bag Simon was holding and his expression changed to one of smug understanding. Instead of saying anything, he just raised his right eyebrow at Simon. Simon glanced at Zack and noticed his cheeks were once again pink. This caused Simon's cock to jerk in his pants. His mate looked sexy as hell when he was trying to hide his embarrassment.

Turning back to his brother, he smiled. "Zack and Hayley are spending the night." With that pronouncement, he grabbed Zack's hand, turned and left the room. He could hear the chuckles follow him as he led Zack down the passageway. Once they reached Simon's room, he turned to talk to Hayley.

"This is my room, Princess. Your daddy will be in here if you need him at any time, okay?" Hayley nodded and snuggled further into Zack's arms. "Would you like to see where you will be sleeping?" Once again the little girl nodded in her daddy's arms.

"See this door right here? This is your room." Simon opened the door next to his and walked inside. The room, being in a house of so many males was extremely masculine. The bed was thick chunky wood with a dark blue quilt and pillows. The chest of draws and bedside table were made to match the bed and gave the room the overall feel of belonging to a man. They would have a lot of changes to make if he could convince Zack and Hayley to move in with him. He knew he wanted his mate with him always but wasn't sure how Zack would feel about living with his brothers.

Simon was aware their living arrangement wasn't the most conventional of set ups but it worked for his family. The brothers had all been close growing up with only a few years between each one, and Simon wasn't sure he wanted to live apart from them yet. His wolf liked living in a large group and living under the same roof as his alpha gave Simon the added sense of security. He would have to talk to Zack about moving in with them and see if he could persuade his mate.

"Wow, look at the bed, you're going to get lost in there tonight." Hayley giggled at her father before he let her down. They watched as she ran across the room then attempted to climb up on the bed. She was just a little too short to be able to heave herself up entirely. Simon went to help and once Hayley was up she climbed right to the middle and settled down with a soft sigh.

"Oh no, you don't, missy. It's shower time. You need to get washed and dressed and brush your teeth. Come on." Hayley reluctantly crawled to the edge of the bed where Zack took her and helped her down. "We'll just be a minute." Zack said to him as he picked up their overnight bag and headed into the attached bathroom.

Simon sat on the edge of the bed to wait. He looked down at the erection currently tenting his pants. "Soon," he muttered. The damn thing wouldn't go away. Simon was lost in thought ten minutes later when Zack emerged from the bathroom with a sleepy looking Hayley in his arms.

"Let's go say goodnight to everyone then we'll tuck you in." Hayley nodded and was let down. She held Zack's hand and in the other she clutched her wolf teddy tightly to her chest. Simon followed them out, He leant against the wall leading into the living room and watched as Hayley said goodnight to his family.

She walked right up to Alex and held her arms out asking for a hug. Alex seemed to be startled by the gesture and didn't know exactly what to do. He looked at Zack and silently asked what she wanted. "She would like to give you a hug goodnight." Zack said softly. Alex, finally understanding, sat forward and picked Hayley up, giving her a gentle hug before putting her back down. The expression on his big Alpha brother's face when he let go of Hayley was so tender and caring; he had never seen his brother look at anyone but his mate like that.

Hayley walked around and gave everyone else a good night hug. Brian seemed to hold her extra long and when he let go, he turned to Marcus and said so quietly Simon could barely hear him, "I want one of these."

"I know, we'll get there," Marcus replied just as quietly.

When Hayley was finished, Simon pushed off the wall. "Goodnight, everyone." He said as he turned and led the way back to Hayley's room. Once she was tucked in tight and a nightlight plugged in for her, Simon leant across the bed and kissed her on the cheek. "Goodnight, Princess."

"Night night, Simon. Night night, Daddy." Simon watched as Zack leant and gave his daughter a big hug and a kiss goodnight.

"If you need us in the night, we're right next door. Okay, Pumpkin?" Hayley nodded but didn't reply as her eyelids were already closing.

Simon took Zack by the hand and they quietly left the room, shutting the door behind them. Once they were in the passageway, Simon couldn't hold back any longer and pushed Zack against the wall. Threading his hands in Zack's hair, he closed the distance between them and brought his lips down against Zack's, devouring his mate's mouth.

The needy little whimpers that escaped from Zack only served to enflame Simon's body. Reaching down he grabbed Zack's hips and pulled him forward so their hard cocks were mashed against each other as he continued to plunder Zack's mouth with his tongue.

Simon could feel Zack's hands pulling on his shirt until he was successful in getting the material released from his pants. The feel of his mate's soft hands against his hard abdomen caused his cock to jerk and leak out a small amount of pre-cum.

The sound of a throat clearing invaded the fog that had filled his brain at the slightest touch from his mate. Reluctantly pulling away from their kiss, Simon looked down at Zack and groaned. His lips were red and kiss swollen with a light sheen of spit coating them. He was panting heavily and his hair was a mess from where Simon had grabbed him. The throat clearing again made Simon turn his head.

Marcus stood not too far from them with a knowing look on his face. "As hot as that was, and it was hotter than hell," Marcus seemed to pause for a second, "get a room!" He then turned and continued on his way.

Simon groaned and rested his forehead against Zack's. "Sorry, babe, but I just couldn't hold off any longer."

"I understand, Simon. How about we take your smart brother's advice?"

"God, don't say that within hearing distance of Marcus. He'll get a big head."

Zack's small giggle was cut off when Simon leant down and kissed him again. "Come on, time to get you naked."

"I couldn't agree more."

Simon stepped back then practically dragged Zack through his bedroom door before closing it behind them. "Naked, now," was all Simon could seem to get himself to say. His brain was misfiring with his mate being this close to him and knowing what they were about to do.

Simon watched as Zack hurried to try and rid himself of his clothing. His mouth was watering as Zack's chest was bared, the small pink nipples hard and wanting. Zack's stomach was nice and flat, he wasn't muscular but Simon didn't care. He had always preferred smaller men to muscular ones. His eyes zeroed in when Zack slid down the zip on his pants, but didn't drop them

Simon trailed his gaze back up Zack's body and finally reached his eyes. "You know this won't work if only one of us is naked?" Zack stated, eyeing Simon's still fully clothed body. Simon laughed then started tugging at his own clothes. Unzipping his pants, he watched as Zack studied his body. He hoped his mate liked what he saw. He wasn't as muscled as either of his other brothers but he did work out and had a nice firm six pack he took pride in.

He let his pants drop and watched as realisation hit Zack; he had gone sans underwear. The needy little whimper that came from Zack caused his cock to bob. He loved the noises his mate made. Zack quickly dropped his own pants and pushed his underwear down. Kicking off his shoes and getting rid of his socks, Zack stood in front of Simon gloriously naked.

Simon's eyes roamed his mate's naked body before coming to a stop at his groin. The hard cock that stood out from Zack's body was probably a good six inches in length and nice and fat. His cock was surrounded by a thatch of neatly trimmed bright red curls. Simon couldn't wait to taste his mate, to feel that thick cock sliding in and out of his mouth.

Growling, Simon reached out and pulled Zack against his body. Simon couldn't have held back the moan that escaped his lips at the first touch of their naked bodies against each other if his life had depended on it. Threading his fingers though Zack's soft silky hair, he pulled his head back until it was tilted to just the right angle where Simon could take possession of those lips again.

Refusing to break the contact their lips had made, Simon slowly started to walk Zack backwards towards the bed. When Zack stopped, he gently pushed and Zack fell on his back onto the bed. Simon followed him down, continuing to rain kisses down on Zack's body as he went.

Working his way down Zack's neck towards his chest, Simon could hear the moans escaping from the redhead. Reaching a small pink nipple, Simon stuck his tongue out and flicked it across the hard nub before taking the small morsel into his mouth and sucking. Biting down gently on the hard nipple, Simon was amazed at Zack's reaction. The loud gasp followed by his back arching off the bed and Zack's hands threading through his hair, pulling his head down against his chest had Simon's cock leaking copious amounts of pre-cum.

Kissing his way across Zack's chest, Simon hungrily bit Zack's other nipple before soothing away the sting with his tongue. Zack writhed and moaned beneath him, thrusting his hips against Simon.

"Simon, please, feels so good." Zack's breathy moans only served to inflame Simon's lust further.

"Shhh babe, I know what you need. Scoot up the bed then lie back and relax." Simon knelt, allowing Zack to move from underneath him. Zack manoeuvred himself to the centre of the bed then settled back against the pillows. His hard cock jutting out proudly from his body, a tiny clear drop of fluid beaded on its head. Simon slowly crawled up his mate's body to continue his exploration, kissing his feet, calves, and thighs as he went.

When he finally reached the hard straining erection bobbing erratically with need, Simon didn't even pause to think; he simply opened his mouth and swallowed the cock to the root. Zack screamed beneath him, thrusting his hips, his cock going deeper down his throat.

Simon pulled back until just the head was held in his mouth. Using his tongue, he flicked it against the slit, tasting the pre-cum that had gathered. Simon groaned as the taste of his mate burst across his tastebuds, Zack was sweet yet spicy with just a hint of tang. Simon lowered his head again then started up a steady rhythm.

Making his way to the tip of Zack's cock, Simon once again dipped his tongue into the slit. The noises coming from Zack only served to add fuel to his fire. Licking down the vein that ran the length of his mate's cock, Simon made his way to the tight hairless balls. Taking them one at a time between his lips, Simon rolled the small orbs around inside his mouth before pulling back as far as he could before letting go.

Sucking two of his fingers into his mouth, Simon's gaze roamed up his mate's flushed body until their eyes met. Zack was still panting hard, his fists clenched in the sheets beneath him. His eyes were half lidded and his lips were still swollen from their earlier kisses. He looked absolutely fucking adorable.

* * * *

Zack's body was going to go up in flames, he just knew it would. Simon's hand sent tingles shooting through his body from the tips of his toes to the top of his head. As he looked down his body at the sight before him, Zack couldn't hold back the pleas as he watched his mate sucking on his fingers, getting them ready to enter his needy body. "Simon…," the name escaped him as more a whisper than anything else but his mate still heard him.

"Lift your legs, babe." Zack hurried to comply, lifting his legs and pulling them back to expose his tight entrance to the man he was quickly falling for. Zack's cock looked obscene between his legs, jutting forward, still wet with Simon's spit, the tip leaking constant pre-cum.

Zack moaned as Simon rubbed a finger around his hole, gently applying pressure before pushing its way inside. His head thrashing back and forth against the pillows beneath him, Zack wanted more. He concentrated on relaxing his body as he didn't want to hinder Simon in any way from getting to where they both wanted to end up.

Feeling the thick finger push all the way into his body before starting its retreat had all sorts of things falling from his lips. "More… Please Simon, I need more… need you… want your cock… hurry."

"Don't want to hurt you," Simon said as he pushed a second finger inside Zack. Zack moaned at the feeling and tried to thrust his hips back against the fingers. Simon thrust them fast and deep a couple of times before bending them and stroking the inside walls of his channel. Zack couldn't help but scream again when Simon's fingers grazed against his sweet spot.

Simon leant forward and swallowed his cock to the root again as he added a third finger to his lover's greedy hole. Zack's hips trust up of their own accord. "I'm ready… please, I don't want to come until you're inside me… I'm so close, Simon."

When Simon pulled back, Zack whimpered at the sudden feeling of being empty. Simon crawled up his body and laid claim to his lips in a kiss that sent his heart racing. They were forced to pull back due to lack of oxygen, and it was then Zack noticed Simon was holding a bottle of lube.

"You ready, babe?"

"Oh yeah, I want that gorgeous cock inside me now."

Simon chuckled as he flipped the lid and squirted a generous amount onto his cock. Zack watched in fascination as Simon gripped his shaft and slowly spread the viscous liquid. He was so fascinated at watching his mate's cock, he jumped in surprise when Simon squirted the cool liquid against his hole.

Zack pulled his legs back again and watched as Simon settled between his legs, his thighs rubbing against Zack's ass cheeks. Simon had a hold of his cock and was gently teasing it against Zack's hole, "Ready?"

"Simon… Now, goddamn it!" All the air left his lungs as Simon seated himself within Zack in one smooth hard thrust. They both moaned at the feeling of finally being joined together the way mates should be.

"So good… so full…," Zack panted as Simon started a slow and gentle thrust.

"So tight, babe… love the way you squeeze my cock. Feels like you're going to burn my dick, you're so hot."

"Harder, Simon! I won't break. Fuck me into the mattress."

"As you wish, babe." Simon leant forward and kissed him, matching his tongue thrusts to those of his cock. Zack let go of his legs and wrapped them around Simon's waist, threading his arms around Simon's neck to hold on.

Simon pulled back and left Zack panting for breath as he quickened his thrusts. Simon's hands pushed Zack's thighs back until he was just about bent double. The quick hard thrusts were forcing him up the bed. Simon was pegging his gland with every thrust and he knew his orgasm wasn't far away.

There was one thing Zack wanted above anything else at that moment and he wanted it before he came. "Bite me."

Simon seemed to pause for a moment before he continued with his rhythm. "Are you sure?"

"Yes, claim me. I want you as my mate for now and forever. Please Simon." Zack turned his head to the side, offering his mate his neck. He knew it was a submissive gesture and had no problem making it to his mate. He watched in awe as Simon lost control. Simon's eyes shifted and his teeth elongated, he could feel his claws start to lengthen as they gripped his hips.

With a loud roar, Simon jammed his cock home and bit into the base of Zack's neck as hot cum flooded his passage. The dual sensations were too much for Zack and he felt himself tip over the edge as wet heat spread between their bodies.

Zack nearly cried out again as the knot extended from Simon and latched onto his prostate. He had completely forgotten about the mating knot. Simon slowly extracted his teeth from his neck and licked the mark closed before leaning over and kissing him to within an inch of his life.

The pleasure was too much for Zack and he felt his body shudder again as he was swept away in another mind blowing orgasm, so powerful his body had no other way to cope but to surrender to the darkness.

Chapter 6

Simon woke feeling as if someone was staring at him. Opening his eyes, he blinked trying to get them to focus. Noticing the light streaming through the gaps in the curtain, he realised it must be morning. Finally able to make his brain work, Simon realised two things at once. He was still completely naked and wrapped around Zack and Hayley was standing at the side of the bed looking at him.

"Good morning, Princess. Did you sleep well?" Simon asked in a whisper while he discreetly moved the sheets to make sure both he and Zack were completely covered. The movement stirred Zack and he rolled over and snuggled deep against Simon's chest, placing a small kiss to his neck. Simon bit back his moan as he realised Hayley was still standing there watching them.

"I'm hungry." The loud voice of a two year old broke through any remaining fog that was lingering from his sleep. Zack seem to startle awake at his daughter's voice and he sat bolt upright, rubbing at his eyes.

"*Easy, babe. Everything's fine.*" Simon couldn't believe how happy he was feeling just from communicating silently with his mate for the first time. *His mate*. He still couldn't believe he had found the man destined to be his.

Zack seemed to calm down at his voice before smiling and turning to kiss him. When he turned back to Hayley, he was wide awake. "Well hello there, Pumpkin. Did you sleep the whole night in that big bed all by yourself?"

Hayley smiled at her daddy before lifting her arms, wanting to be picked up. Zack made sure he was covered before lifting Hayley up on the bed and into his lap. Zack kissed Hayley on the cheek and Simon decided he should get in on the action as well. Scooting over he placed a big wet sloppy good morning kiss on Hayley's cheek as well.

The little girl squealed and giggled in her daddy's arms. "Scratchy," Hayley said as she rubbed at her cheek.

"So I hear you're hungry?"

"Yep!"

"Yes, Hayley, not yep."

"Sorry, Daddy."

"It's okay. Go wait outside and Simon and I will get dressed then we can all have some breakfast."

"Okay, Daddy." Hayley said as she climbed from her daddy's lap before sliding off the bed and running for the door.

Once Hayley had left the room, Zack turned to Simon. "Now, where's my good morning kiss?" Simon, still not believing he had found this man, scooted forward and laid a kiss exactly like the one he had on Hayley on Zack's cheek.

"Urgh!" Zack laughed as he pulled away from Simon."I'll get you for that."

Simon couldn't help but laugh as he jumped from the bed and ran to the bathroom. Before he could reach the door, Zack caught him and pinned him against the wall.

"Now this feels familiar." Zack's voice was a low sultry purr and Simon felt his dick get hard immediately. "Now, where is my proper good morning kiss from my mate? I'm not leaving until I get one."

"That doesn't really entice me to kiss you good morning, babe. I would be quite happy to stay right here with you all day, naked and hard." Simon punctuated his words with a thrusting of his hips.

"As much as I would love to, we have a little girl who would like some food." Simon knew this, so he gave in and kissed his mate good morning. The kiss was slow and unhurried, a gentle melding of tongues and lips. When they finally broke apart, Simon stared Zack in the eyes, as happy as he had ever been in his life.

"Good morning, babe."

Zack's smile lit up his whole face. *"Good morning*

to you too. Now let's get dressed."

* * * *

Zack was walking on cloud nine as he made his way through Simon's house looking for Hayley. He knew he had a big goofy grin on his face but didn't care. Reaching up, he gently ran his fingers over the mark Simon had left on him last night. Zack shivered as the touch sent electric currents racing through his body.

Walking into the kitchen, Zack stopped as everyone seated around the table turned and looked at him. Zack realised he was still lightly fingering his bite mark and lowered his hand, his face heating at being caught. Strong arms wrapped around his waist from behind and he was pulled back against a hard chest.

Zack's body turned to mush and he moaned at being held in Simon's arms. Simon nuzzled into his neck and kissed his mating mark. Zack's knees gave out and, if it wasn't for Simon's arms around him, he would have ended up an embarrassing puddle on the floor.

"*You okay there, babe?"*

"Uh huh." Simon chuckled then kissed him again before making sure he was steady on his feet and stepping away.

"Come on, time to get something to eat. Would you

like some coffee?"

"Huh?" Zack was still having difficulty getting his brain to recognise any sort of higher communication as tingles still raced through his muscles.

"Coffee?" Simon asked again and laughed. "Why don't you sit down, babe?"

Sitting? Now that he could do. Zack made his way to the table and sat next to Hayley who was currently on what looked to be her second piece of toast with vegemite. The crusts were scattered over the plate and table and Zack was sure she had more vegemite on her face than in her mouth.

Looking at his daughter, Zack finally got control of his body. "Look at you. You're a mess again. Last night a tomato sauce monster and this morning a vegemite monster!" Simon placed a steaming cup of coffee in front of him and Zack took it with thanks.

"Okay guys, breakfast is ready. Can someone help me with all this?" Brian called out from the kitchen

Zack looked at Simon, wanting to know what was going on.

"Brian does most of the cooking around here as we're all pretty much hopeless at anything like that. We usually have a cooked breakfast on the weekends since we all have a little more time than we do during the week. Plus we generally get to go running and burn of all the calories."

Zack smiled wistfully at the thought of going running. He hadn't been able to let his wolf out and go for a run in at least six months if not longer. Ever since Sarah had died and her parents had started their vendetta against him, Zack hadn't trusted anyone else to look after his daughter. So he had put his needs and, those of his wolf, to the side and concentrated on raising his little girl.

"Everything okay?" Zack couldn't believe how attuned to him Simon seemed to be already.

"Yeah, just would love to be able to go running as a wolf. It's been a while."

"How long's a while, Zack?"

"Umm. Over six months."

"Jesus, really?" Everyone in the room turned to look at Simon at his sudden outburst. Zack just nodded his head, too embarrassed to answer. When everyone realised nothing else was going to be forthcoming, they all turned back to what they were doing.

"Don't worry, we'll sort something out." Simon leaned in to whisper in his ear. All conversation was then stopped as the food was placed on the table and everyone dug in. Zack cut up some sausage to let it cool down and placed them in amongst all the crusts on Hayley's plate.

"I don't think I can eat this." Brian said suddenly.

"Baby, are you okay?" Marcus asked. Zack looked up and noticed Brian was looking rather pale. Brian shook his head before covering his mouth quickly and running from the room. Marcus swiftly followed behind him.

Zack wondered what was wrong with him; being a werewolf they very rarely got sick as their bodies were immune to most human diseases. Wondering if he should ask, he noticed every head at the table looking at the door that Brian and Marcus had just gone through.

"Is everything okay with Brian?" Zack decided it couldn't hurt to ask.

"I'm not sure, babe." Simon answered his question and wrapped an arm around his shoulders.

Breakfast after that was a quiet affair; Brian and Marcus didn't rejoin them. Once everyone had eaten at least half their plates and downed god knows how much coffee, they all seemed to regain a little vibrancy.

"So Simon, it's your turn today." Alex said with a little too much enjoyment for Zack's liking.

Simon groaned next to him and seemed to deflate in his seat a little. What the hell were these people talking about? Simon saw the obvious confusion on his face and explained.

"I already told you Brian does the cooking here." Zack nodded and Simon continued "Since Brian does all the cooking, we now have the problem of grocery shopping, and none of us like doing it. So to make things fair, there's a list on the fridge. You write whatever is needed and we take it in turns to do the shopping. This way, we each only have to do the shopping once a month which isn't too bad, but as Alex and Jason did it last week, he thought he would rub it in that he's done for another three weeks and it's my turn."

Zack laughed at what his mate had said. Seriously, they used a schedule for doing the shopping? How the hell had they survived before Brian arrived? He couldn't believe four huge strapping brothers were so hopeless when it came to household chores. He'd been doing his own cooking, cleaning and ironing since he moved out of home and in with Sarah.

Zack was still chuckling when he leant over and gave Simon a kiss on the cheek. "Don't worry, Hayley and I will go with you so the big bad supermarket doesn't scare you."

Simon's cheeks heated and everyone else at the table laughed before going back to their breakfasts.

"You'll pay for that, but thank you." Simon growled in his ear before kissing him.

Things definitely wouldn't be dull around here that was sure, Zack though before he picked up his knife and fork and finished his breakfast.

CHAPTER 7

Simon hated shopping with a capital H. But he had to admit it was a hell of a lot nicer doing the dreaded chore with Zack and Hayley than it was by himself. Hayley sat in the front of the trolley chattering away to herself while Simon pushed and Zack consulted the shopping list they had been given. Hayley constantly pointed things out on the shelves she wanted and every so often Simon would sneak one of the items into the trolley when Zack wasn't looking, much to Hayley's delight.

Simon had an uneasy feeling ever since they'd left home this morning. The back of his neck was tickling like he could feel someone watching, but he'd been unable to see anyone who looked suspicious. He didn't want to alarm Zack yet, after everything he'd been through, he deserved a break.

Turning around when he felt like daggers were being stared at him, he just caught someone ducking around the end of the aisle. Not sure if the person was simply another shopper, Simon wasn't going to take that chance and leave Zack and Hayley by themselves. He would mention his feelings and thoughts to Alex when his brother got home from work this afternoon.

They finally finished and were loading the groceries into the back of Zack's car when he felt it again. Looking around he noticed a couple in their early fifties driving down the street, staring straight at him and not at the road. They sped off before Simon had a chance to ask Zack if he knew who they were. Simon didn't like this one bit. He had a feeling he knew exactly who the couple was. He would have to ask Zack what the Stewarts looked liked.

Once they were home and the groceries were put away, they inquired about Brian. Today was one of Marcus's rare Saturdays off and Simon was thankful for that since he couldn't help but think Marcus would be driving himself sick with worry if he'd had to go to work while his mate was ill.

Marcus informed them Brian was in bed and resting. He was feeling extremely nauseous and was having trouble keeping anything down so Marcus had tucked him in and told him to try and get some sleep. Simon could hear the worry in his brother's voice. Hopefully it would sort itself out soon and Brian would be his normal happy self again.

Lunch was once more a quiet affair. Alex came home to check on things and have a quick bite to eat before he had to go back to work. Simon didn't get an opportunity to talk with him about his suspicions regarding the Stewarts, he hoped it could wait until tonight when he finished work.

Once they put Hayley down for her afternoon nap, Simon walked into the living room where Rick and Jason were situated in front of the television watching the afternoon football game. "Hey guys." Simon said as he entered, pulling Zack along behind him.

"Hey, what's up?"

"Nothing much, would you mind keeping an ear out for Hayley? She's just gone down for her nap and, hopefully, should be out for a couple of hours. I just wanted to take Zack for a run since he hasn't had a chance to let his wolf out in a long time."

Simon could feel the anticipation just about rolling off Zack as they waited for confirmation from his brothers.

"Yeah, no worries. Hayley's a little angel, so shouldn't be any trouble if she wakes. Just be careful since it's the middle of the day. We don't want anyone to see you." Rick replied.

"Thanks, little brother. Don't worry, we'll be careful." Zack was practically vibrating standing next to him.

"Thank you, thank you, thank you!" Zack said

excitedly from beside him. Simon could just imagine what Zack was feeling at the moment. His wolf had to be close to the surface, knowing it was going to get a chance to get out and run soon.

"We shouldn't be more than an hour, hour and a half." Simon said as he started to lead Zack from the room.

"Take your time and enjoy. Don't worry about anything here. Marcus and Brian are still here as well."

Simon led Zack into the garage and motioned Zack to get in his car. Once they were on the road to the pack land, Zack seemed to calm a little. Simon, remembering earlier this morning, kept a keen eye on his rear-view mirror to make sure no one followed them. Not seeing any sign of the Stewarts, or anyone else, Simon relaxed and enjoyed the drive with his mate.

Pulling up in the car park Simon parked the car and got out. He walked to the front and waited for Zack to join him.

"Usually we undress here. But as it's the middle of the day, how about we walk into the pack meeting area and we can shift there?" Simon asked. There weren't any other cars in the car park but you could never be too careful when it came to keeping their secret.

"Sounds good. Let's go." Zack said as he grabbed

Simon's hand and started dragging him towards the bush. Simon laughed and pulled against Zack's hand. His enthusiasm was catching.

"It's this way, babe." Simon said, pointing in a completely different direction to the one Zack was leading him in.

"Well, lead the way then. We don't have all day." Zack laughed. Simon led the way through the bush and they were soon at the pack's meeting grounds. By the time Simon turned around to look at Zack, his mate was already out of his shirt and was working on his pants, having kicked off his shoes. Simon couldn't help but laugh.

"A little anxious, babe?"

"Yeah, a little. Sorry. But if I don't undress, I'm not going to have any clothes to wear home. I don't think I can hold him off much longer."

"It's okay. Go ahead and shift. I know how long it's been for you."

"Thanks." Zack didn't get a chance to say anything else as the change swept over him. Watching someone change always fascinated Simon. To see the fur erupting along his skin and the bones disjointing and reshaping, was mesmerising to watch. Simon knew exactly what Zack was feeling as he let his wolf have free reign over his body.

In less than a minute Zack, the man he was quickly falling in love with, was no longer standing in front of him. Instead he was left facing the most breathtakingly beautiful red wolf he had ever seen.

Zack's coat was a mixture of reds and oranges with flecks of brown running through it. The colours made it look like his coat was on fire and Simon had never seen anything so beautiful in his life. He couldn't think of any other word but 'stunning' to describe how his mate looked in his wolf form. Simon knew he was staring but he couldn't take his eyes off the beauty in front of him.

It wasn't until Zack walked up to him and nudged him that the spell was broken and Simon was able to gather his thoughts once again. *"You are the most gorgeous creature I have ever seen."* Simon conveyed with awc as hc started to get undressed.

The wolf in front of him seemed to huff then leant forward to lick his hand before sitting back on its haunches and cocking his head to the side, waiting. Simon got the message and quickly divested himself of the rest of his clothes.

Once he was naked, Simon allowed the change to take over. His skin started to tingle, signifying the start of the change, fur sprouted all over his body and his bones popped and reshaped themselves. Within moments, he was on all fours and couldn't be happier. Walking up to his mate who was still sitting and watching him, Simon noticed he was larger than Zack in this form as well. He licked Zack's muzzle before dipping his head a little and gently biting his neck. Zack sat still the entire time Simon rubbed up against him, marking his mate with his scent.

Once Simon was happy he had marked his mate for all to smell, he stepped back. "*Come on, babe, let's run.*" Zack didn't need any more encouragement than that and took off towards the bush, leaving Simon behind. Simon huffed and took off after his mate, the scent of the bush filling Simon's lungs as he ran. He never got sick of this area. There was always something new to see, from the Banksia flowers and wild orchards to the large eucalyptus trees. This bushland had been his home for his entire life and Simon couldn't imagine living anywhere else.

Nipping at Zack's heels, Simon got his attention before leading him through the bush to a small creek. They sat and lapped at the water like an animal dying of thirst before taking off once again. They playfully chased a couple of rabbits, not wanting to catch them as they had no reason to kill; they were not hungry and didn't need to eat.

When Simon decided they had been out long

enough, he led Zack back to the clearing so they could change and go home. Simon stopped next to their clothes and once again allowed the change to flow through his body. Standing naked in the middle of the clearing and looking at his equally naked mate had Simon's cock rock hard in seconds.

Zack ran and jumped on him wrapping his arms and legs around Simon's body. Simon staggered under the additional weight but was able to keep his feet. "Oh, thank you, thank you, this place is wonderful," Zack said as he peppered Simon's face and neck with kisses.

"You're welcome, babe." Simon wrapped one hand around the nape of his mate's neck and pulled him down for a proper kiss. Taking control, he thrust his tongue into Zack's mouth and moaned as the unique flavour of his mate burst onto his tongue.

Simon could feel Zack's cock harden against his stomach and wanted nothing more than to take his mate here and now. However, he didn't want to hurt Zack and he hadn't thought to bring any lube. He wouldn't be making that mistake again. Pulling away from the questing, eager tongue of his mate, Simon smacked him on the ass, "Down, babe."

Zack's face fell as he lowered his legs from around

Simon's body and stepped back. "You look cute when you pout," Simon whispered in Zack's ear before placing a quick kiss on his lips and turning away. Simon grabbed the clothes on the ground, but instead of handing them to Zack, he laid them out on the ground to form a crude blanket.

Turning back to Zack he held his hand out for his mate. The smile that split Zack's face when he realised what Simon was doing made his whole face light up. Zack placed his hand in Simon's and allowed Simon to manoeuvre him to where he wanted. Once Zack was splayed out on the clothes to Simon's satisfaction, he dropped to his knees between Zack's spread legs.

He ran his hand's lightly up and down Zack's trembling legs. Crawling over his mate, Simon was soon looking into the eyes of the man he would spend the rest of his life making happy. Zack's hands gently rubbed up and down his back and Simon felt his emotions just under the surface as if they were a living breathing thing and wanted to get out.

This beautiful man under him was all his. Everything Zack had been though just went to show how strong his mate was and made Simon love him even more. He would do anything to protect his mate and their daughter and make sure there was nothing but happiness in their lives from now on.

Simon lowered himself and gently kissed the one he loved. This kiss was gentle and sweet, a melding of lips and tongue. Simon hoped the kiss conveyed everything he was feeling, but just in case it didn't, he pulled away. Gazing once again into those beautiful hazel eyes, he wanted to let Zack know how he felt and prayed it wasn't too soon for his mate.

"I love you, Zack." Simon whispered. He watched as Zack's eyes widened a moment before a smile lit his features.

"I love you too, Simon." Simon was so happy he thought his heart would burst.

"Move in with me, please?" Simon figured he may as well go for broke, he wanted his mate and their little girl with him always and the thought of them living somewhere other than with him was painful.

The wary expression Zack now wore said he needed a little convincing and Simon was more than happy to do it. "Please, babe? I want you and Hayley with me always. We can re-do the spare room to make the place a more kid friendly one. We can even paint the room pink if you'd like. The guys love her already and it's calming to live with pack. Please just say you'll think about it at least?"

Zack nodded then kissed him again and all thoughts fled from Simon's head as his mate took possession of his mouth. Simon broke the kiss several minutes later and started to work his way down Zack's body. After having their hard cocks rubbing against each other while kissing, Simon was going out of his mind with want.

Kissing his way across Zack's flat stomach, Simon was finally where he wished to be. Flicking his tongue out, he lapped up the clear drop of pre-cum that had beaded on the head of Zack's cock. Once the flavour hit Simon, he wanted more and swallowed Zack down whole.

Zack screamed and thrust his hips, pushing his cock further down Simon's throat. Simon pressed his hips back to the ground to still his movements and continued a steady rhythm up and down Zack's prick.

"Simon, please. I want to taste you too." The breathless moan came from above him. Now that was an idea Simon could get on board with. Not wanting to let go of his prize, Simon swung his body around and manoeuvred his legs so they rested on either side of Zack's head.

The feeling of his cock being engulfed in wet heat caused him to moan around the length that was still in his mouth. This caused a reaction from Zack and Simon could soon feel the vibrations running the length of his cock as Zack moaned or groaned or cried out, he couldn't tell which. Moving one of his hands, Simon gently cupped Zack's balls and swirled them in his fingers. The other hand he brought to his mouth and sucked two fingers alongside the cock he was happily sucking on. Once his fingers were good and wet, he made his way to the hot clenching hole that was just waiting to be filled.

Pulling back on the cock in his mouth, Simon concentrated on sucking on the head and spearing his tongue in and out of the slit gathering all the pre-cum he could. Running his finger around Zack's hole several times, he waited until the muscles loosened then pressed forward. He was immediately sucked unto the tight velvety walls of his mate's ass. Spearing his finger in and out several times seemed to drive Zack wild. He bucked his hips several times before screaming.

The cock in his mouth pulsed, and burst after burst of his mate's cum filled his mouth. Groaning at the taste, Simon couldn't hold back any longer and thrust his hips towards Zack's mouth and let his own orgasm take over as he swallowed down his mate's thick, tangy release.

Once Zack had finished coming, Simon licked his cock clean determined to get every last drop of his mate's essence. Pulling away, he swung his leg over and collapsed on the ground next to his mate; they were both breathing heavily.

Their hands found each other and they lay there, in the middle of the pack clearing, sun shining down on their sated, naked bodies and held hands while they tried to recover from what had just happened.

"Okay, we'll move in with you on one condition." Zack said after several minutes of nothing but heavy breathing.

Simon's heart leapt for joy at his mate's words. He didn't care what the condition was, he would do anything to make Zack and Hayley happy. "Anything, babe."

Zack giggled. "I want a repeat of that."

"Now?" Simon wasn't sure if he was up to going again so soon, but he would give it a good try.

"I don't think I could, even if I wanted to." Zack giggle again. "No, I just mean I want several repeats of that at home."

"Your wish is my command. But at the moment, I think it's time we got dressed and headed home. Hayley should be up soon." Zack groaned but got to his feet. Once they were both dressed they made their way, hand in hand, back through the bush and to Simon's car.

CHAPTER 8

Pulling into the street, all of Zack's euphoric feelings from his run and the amazing sex he and Simon experienced fled. In front of the house there was a car parked that Zack didn't recognise. He had a bad feeling about this, though. As they got closer to the house, Zack's feelings were confirmed as he recognised the couple standing at the door, trying to push their way inside.

Simon growled in the seat next to him; Zack just wanted to get the car parked so he could go and make sure Hayley was safe. Not taking his eyes off the pair currently trying their best to get into the house, Zack jumped from the car when Simon pulled into the garage. Yanking the door open, Zack ran into the house. "Where is she?" he yelled.

Jason poked his head down the passageway. "Calm down, Zack. She's in the kitchen with me having some ice cream." Zack didn't stop on his way to get to Hayley. He had to make sure she was safe with his own eyes. Finding her at the table just as Jason had said, making a mess with ice cream, Zack finally took a breath and allowed his heart to slow down. Walking up to his daughter, he picked her up and crushed her to his chest.

Simon came in and hugged her from behind, pulling Zack into his arms as well.

"Hi, Daddy."

"Hey, Pumpkin. Did you have a nice nap?"

"Yep. I got ice cream," Hayley said brightly, pointing at her rather large bowl of chocolate ice cream. Hayley's smile slowly faded from her face. "Mummy's mummy and daddy are here," she said quietly. Zack's heart broke at everything his little girl had been through. Why wouldn't these people just leave him alone?

"Yes, sweetheart, not yep. And I know, but don't worry. You're safe. They are never going to take you away from me. You stay here and finish your ice cream with Jason. Simon and I will go sort everything out." Zack and Simon both kissed her on the cheek before Zack put her back in the chair at the table. Hayley immediately picked up her spoon and dug it back into her rapidly melting ice cream.

"Would you mind keeping an eye on her?" Zack asked Jason.

"No worries. She's safe here." Zack nodded. Simon took his hand and squeezed it before leading them through the house to the front door. Rick was currently blocking their paths but Zack could clearly hear the filth coming from both Valerie and Howard as they tried to gain entrance to the house.

"Rick, would you, please, be so kind as to go and get Marcus. I know Brian's sick but we might need him." Simon asked from next to him.

Rick nodded then growled once at the couple on the doorstep. Both Valerie and Howard took a step back at the animalistic sound coming from the man in front of them. With a satisfied smile, Rick turned and left to go get Marcus.

"What are you doing here, Howard, Valerie? We've been through this and the courts gave me full custody."

"The courts were wrong. You're a disgusting pervert and you don't deserve to have a child." Valerie sneered at him. Simon snarled and took a menacing step forward. Zack caught his wrist to stop him from going too far. The Stewarts took yet another step backwards.

"Just let us take Hayley and you'll never see us again." Howard added.

"Hayley is my daughter and you have no right to try and take her from me. If you even try to, I will have you arrested."

"Just try it. No one would believe a filthy homo like you anyway."

"I would." Marcus said from behind Zack.

"And who the bloody hell are you? Another homo?" Valerie asked.

"I am Police Inspector Marcus Holland." Marcus answered as he showed them his badge. "And I suggest you get back in your car and leave before I arrest you both for trespassing, attempted kidnapping, breaching a court order and anything else I can think of. Oh and, yes, I am also gay." Marcus smiled at the pair.

Zack could just kiss him, but thought now might not be the best time.

"You can't do that." Howard said, sounding a lot more confident than he looked.

"Yes, as a matter of fact, I can. And I will do it, with pleasure, if you so much as come anywhere near this town again. I suggest you folks get back in your car and go home and forget all about Zack and Hayley. If you don't, I will come down on you like a tonne of bricks and make sure you both serve time in prison."

Simon had moved up during Marcus's speech until the brothers were standing next to one another, arms crossed over their chests, looking very intimidating. Zack noticed another car pull up to the curb and wondered who else was coming to join the party.

"You haven't heard the last from us, Zack." Valerie said as she pulled on Howard's arm.

"Yes, he has, unless you really have a hankering for prison life."

Joe and Maryanne had made their way up the path to the front door by this time.

"Where's our little girl?" Maryanne was just about bubbling over with excitement at getting to see Hayley again and Zack couldn't help but break out in a smile.

"She's in the kitchen stuffing her face with ice cream at the moment." Simon replied.

Valerie and Howard stopped in their retreat to face Joe and Maryanne. "Don't tell me you're okay with that sick homo raising an innocent child!" Maryanne sucked in a breath at the hateful words. Joe however didn't ever bat an eyelid. He simply cocked his fist back and let fly. Right into Howard's nose. Howard screamed like a girl and crumpled to the ground.

"You watch how you talk about my son." Joe scowled, looking down at the simpering figure Howard made on the ground. Zack was nearly gleeful. He wanted to jump up and down and clap his hands at the same time. He could hear a little snicker escape from one of the men standing next to him but wasn't sure which as they had both schooled their features quickly.

"Zack's not your son. His parents are dead." Valerie practically screamed at Joe as she tried to help Howard up off the ground.

"He's as good as. Now if you don't mind, I have a grandbaby to go and spoil." Maryanne said before she turned her back on the pair and walked up to the men standing in front of the door.

Zack didn't know what to say. He simply stepped forward and kissed her on the cheek. "Thank you." He whispered in her ear.

Maryanne patted his cheek a couple of times before she spoke. "You're family now, Zack. That's all there is to it." Zack nodded and let her into the house.

"Officer, that's assault, I want to press charges." Howard was once again on his feet, his face dripping with blood. Zack wondered if Joe had broken his nose or not.

"Sorry," Marcus said. "I'm not sure what you're talking about. I didn't see a thing. Did you Simon, Zack?"

"Nope, sorry." Simon said. "I must have been looking the other way."

"No, I was more interested in watching the grass grow." Zack added.

Marcus laughed before turning back to the couple

on their lawn. "I suggest you leave now." He then turned and walked into the house followed by Joe, Simon and Zack.

Zack closed the door behind him and leant back against the hard wood closing his eyes. God, he hoped this was over now. Zack opened his eyes as he felt a hand come down on his shoulder.

"Don't worry about it, Zack. I think they got the message, and if not, if they as much as sneeze your way, I will do as I said and arrest the pair of them. Now excuse me, I have a sick mate to get back to."

"How is Brian?"

"A little better than this morning but he's still feeling quite nauseous. I just wish I knew what was causing it."

"Thanks for all your help. And try not to worry too much. I'm sure Brian is going to be fine." Marcus nodded before turning and making his way up the stairs.

Zack made his way through the house to the kitchen where his new family awaited him.

CHAPTER 9

Simon rolled over as the sun streamed through their bedroom window. He had just the right way to wake his mate this morning and, reaching into the bedside table drawer, searched until he came up with what he wanted.

Pulling the lube out, he quietly opened the bottle before rolling back to his side and snuggling up against Zack's back. Simon gently moved his hand under the sheets and manoeuvred his mate's top leg forward, opening Zack's hole to his questing fingers. Pouring slick on his hand, Simon quickly applied the liquid to his straining erection before rubbing his fingers over Zack's hole.

Simon pushed two fingers deep into Zack's warm welcoming body, finding him still stretched from their previous night's lovemaking. Simon quickly added a third finger and, after he was satisfied he wouldn't hurt Zack, he removed his fingers and lined his cock up.

Slowly pushing forward, his cockhead breached the ring of muscles and he stilled, allowing Zack's body to get used to him. Zack moaned and pushed back against him until Simon was seated fully, his balls resting against Zack's ass cheeks. *"Hmmm, Morning, baby, feels good."*

"I love the ways you wake me up." Zack said

sleepily. Simon chuckled. They had been living together for two weeks now. So far Simon had woken Zack with a blow job, by rimming him, he had even, one morning, tied Zack's hands to the bed with his silk ties and run a feather over his entire body driving him crazy, finally making slow love to him.

Simon looked forward to thinking up new and exciting ways to continue to wake his mate for the rest of their lives, but for now he was going to enjoy what he had started. Simon slowly pulled out until just the head of his dick was held in place before slamming forward again.

Zack grunted and moaned and pushed back again for more. Simon set up a steady pace and reached around Zack to wrap his hand around to his mate's hard leaking cock. It only took three strokes before Zack was turning his head and biting the pillow to stop from screaming and ropes of cum shot from his cock.

The feeling of Zack's muscles contracting and clamping down on his cock was enough for Simon; he leant forward and sank his canines into Zack's neck, then followed his mate into orgasmic bliss. Simon continued to stroke Zack as the knot extended and clamped onto his prostate. Zack screamed into the pillow once again as his body erupted for the second time before going limp beneath

Simon.

Pulling away, Simon licked the mark he had made and pulled Zack close as they waited for the knot to recede. The last two weeks had been the happiest of Simon's life. Zack and Hayley had officially moved in. They'd turned the spare room into a room any little girl would be proud of. Simon was right and there was pink everywhere, but the colour didn't bother him as long as Hayley was happy. Zack had started his job at the school and so far seemed to be enjoying it.

Feeling the knot give way, Simon kissed Zack's cheek before popping him on the ass.

"Come on, lazy bones, shower time. You can't spend all day in bed."

Zack grunted before he rolled over and reluctantly followed Simon into the bathroom. After a quick shower and shave, they got dressed and joined the rest of the family for breakfast.

Hayley was already up and at the table having her morning vegemite on toast. Looking around, he noticed Marcus and Brian were missing. They hadn't found out what was wrong with Brian, he was still having trouble keeping some foods down. Marcus was trying to top him up with Gatorade in order to get some electrolytes into him but even they seemed to come up eventually. Alex mentioned it to the pack last night at the full moon gathering. They were hoping someone might know what was going on.

By mid-morning everyone but Marcus and Brian were gathered in the lounge room. Hayley was lying on the floor colouring in one of the books Simon's mum had gotten for her when the doorbell rang.

Rick went to answer and a few minutes later he walked back into the room followed by a couple who Simon recognised as pack members. Tegan was carrying a small baby, who couldn't be more than a couple of months old if that. They stopped and bowed their heads in submission.

"Alpha, sorry to interrupt your Sunday at home." Alex got up from where he was sitting before walking over to them and acknowledging their respect to his position.

"That's okay, Mitchell, Tegan. You're not interrupting anything more exciting than the television. How can we help you?"

Tegan looked at Mitchell then nodded. "Umm. We might know what's wrong with Brian." Mitchell stated quietly. Everyone in the room seemed to sit up straight at that.

"I think I'll go see if Marcus and Brian can join us." Rick, who was still standing with Mitchell and Tegan, headed out of the room.

"Why don't you take a seat?" Alex offered them the couch where he and Jason had been sitting. Alex sat back down in one of the recliners and Jason took up position on his lap. Once everyone seemed to be settled, a quiet descended on the room as they waited for the others to join them.

Less than five minutes later Rick walked in and took a seat on the couch with Zack and Simon. He was followed by Marcus who was carrying a very pale looking Brian in his arms. They settled in the other recliner and all eyes once again turned to the visitors.

"Boy or girl?" Zack broke the silence from beside Simon.

Mitchell had a sad smile on his face as he looked down at the little baby held in his mate's arms. "Boy, Lucas James, named after his fathers."

"Fathers, as in plural?" Alex asked in confusion.

"Yes, my brother, Lucas, and his mate, James. They were killed four weeks ago when their Alpha found out James had given birth to this little one here."

Simon did a double-take at that. Looking around the

room, everyone else seemed to be in the same state of shock that he was. Both Alex and Jason had their mouths hanging open.

"Umm. Excuse me?" Brian squeaked, his voice not hiding his astonishment and fear at what he had just heard. "Did you just say *James* gave birth?"

Mitchell nodded. "As there aren't many gay werewolves, I guess it's not a widely known fact. We certainly didn't know anything about this until I got the call from Lucas to let us know what was going on. Unfortunately, that's all I know. But I reckon if you went to the shops and got a pregnancy test, it would come back positive."

Brian seemed to take all of this in before he looked down at his belly. He gently laid a hand on his stomach and started to cry. Marcus placed his hand over Brian's and kissed him on the forehead, pulling him close. Simon could see silent tears make their way down Marcus's cheeks too.

"Thank you for coming and telling us. I don't have to tell you to please keep this news to yourselves for the time being." Alex spoke quietly into the room.

"Not at all, Alpha, we'll leave you and your family to get used to the news. Sorry we couldn't have been more help." Mitchell and Tegan stood, ready to leave.

"You've been more than helpful. Thank you once again and we're sorry for your loss." They nodded and Rick showed them out the door before coming back.

"Well, that was unexpected." Simon couldn't help but laugh at Jason's comment. It was the understatement of the century if you asked him.

"You know, we're all here for you if you need us, Brian, Marcus." Alex said.

"Thanks. If you don't mind, I think I'll take Brian back to bed so he can rest." Alex nodded his acceptance and Marcus stood, still holding his mate in his arms and walked out the door.

Simon was having a little trouble trying to wrap his head completely around what they had all just learnt. "How the hell did this happen? And why doesn't every werewolf, gay or straight, know about this?" Simon found himself saying to the suddenly quiet room.

No one knew the answer to his questions.

"Oh shit!" Simon spun around at Jason's exclamation.

"What's the matter?" Alex asked his mate

"Does this mean we all have to start using condoms? 'Cause I've got to tell you that's going to get expensive." Alex growled at his mate and pulled him into his lap.

"Never, there will never be a barrier between you and me, you hear?" The Alpha's deep voice rumbled before he pulled his mate into a scorching kiss. Simon, however, saw the brief flash of uncertainly in his brother's eyes.

Simon hadn't even had time to think about the repercussions of not using condoms, his brain was a jumbled mess at the moment. Could he and Zack have children? Was Zack, at this very point in time, pregnant? Did they want to add more to their family? Simon's runaway thoughts were interrupted by his brother.

"After that revelation, I think I have some phone calls to make. Not the least of which is to mum and dad." Alex stood and headed out of the room, quietly followed by a slightly dazed looking Jason.

Simon could just imagine what his parents would say. The next few months were certainly going to be interesting. Wrapping his arm around Zack, he pulled him close and kissed his forehead. Zack gently patted his stomach, trying to comfort him.

"Everything will work out, you'll see." Simon had no doubt his mate was right. Whatever the future held for them, as long as Zack was by his side, he could handle it.

FORBIDDEN MATE
HOLLAND BROTHERS, BOOK FOUR

Rick Holland has watched as his brothers settled into mated bliss, quietly dying inside knowing he will never have the same. Rick has lived for the last ten years with the knowledge his mate doesn't want him. When his brother and Alpha asks him to take a trip, will Rick have the courage to forget his hurt and move on with his life?

Jake Richmond has watched from the sidelines as his mate grew from a surprisingly sexy sixteen year old into a stunningly handsome man. He's done everything within his power to keep that man safe--aware that his mate believes he's not wanted but unable to reveal the truth. Can Jake finally let go of the man he loves or will everything come crashing down when the pair are thrust together in their search for much needed answers?

FORBIDDEN

Mate

THE HOLLAND BROTHERS, BOOK 4

TONI GRIFFIN

SILVER PUBLISHING
Published by Silver Publishing
Publisher of Erotic Romance

Dedication

To my readers: Who have waited patiently, (well, mostly) since the beginning for Patrick and Jake's story. Thank you all for making this an amazing experience. I hope you enjoy.

Lastly to my editor Jason: Thank you for not running away screaming when you receive my manuscripts.

Trademarks Acknowledgement

The author acknowledges the trademarked status and trademark owners of the following wordmarks mentioned in this work of fiction:

Kindle: Amazon Technologies, Inc.
Qantas: Qantas Airways Limited
Mitsubishi: Mitsubishi Motors Corporation
Toyota: Toyota Motor Corporation
Band-Aid: Johnson & Johnson
Bluetooth: Bluetooth SIG, Inc. Corporation

Chapter 1

Jake pulled his car to a stop in front of his best friend's house. Looking around he made note of the cars that were parked in the driveway and on the road. It looked to be quite the full house. Alex, his best friend and his Alpha, had called him last week to let him know they'd found out what was wrong with Brian. Jake had just taken a sip of his coffee when Alex had told him Brian was pregnant. Jake had choked and ended up spraying his desk and all his paperwork with the contents from his mouth.

"You're kidding me, right?" Jake had asked while he frantically grabbed tissues to try and blot the coffee from his desktop.

"Nah man, I'm not." Alex sighed into the phone. His friend sounded tired.

"Nice one, mate, just one problem though—" Jake was seriously starting to think his friend was either playing some type of joke on him or losing his mind, he was hoping for the former.

"Men can't get pregnant?" Alex finished his sentence for him.

"Got it in one." Jake forced a chuckle.

"Yeah, well I was under the same assumption until

yesterday. Brian just took like three different pregnancy tests to confirm it though." Jake didn't know what to say. How could a guy get pregnant?

"How?" He finally managed to squeeze out of his tight throat.

"Well, I assume it's the same for everyone. Insert Tab A into Slot B."

"Asshole, you know what I mean." Jake couldn't help but laugh at Alex's sex-ed lesson though.

"Apparently it has something to do with our condition." Jake sucked in his breath. They were always careful when they were in public about discussing were-creatures since the world didn't know they existed. "I'm still in the process of trying to track down someone who can give me the answers we need."

Jake nodded knowing full well that Alex couldn't see him. His mind was all over the place at the moment. Was it something specific to Brian and Marcus or could it happen to anyone? Would Patrick get pregnant if he settled down with someone or did you have to be mates? Jake growled at the thought of his Patrick pregnant with someone else's child.

"Jake—you okay, man? I know this is a lot to handle but I might need your help if I can get a hold of someone who might know about this."

Shit. Jake couldn't believe he let himself think about Patrick like that while he was talking to Alex. As far as he was aware, Alex had no idea that his little brother was Jake's mate. Shaking his head to try and clear his thoughts, he couldn't let Alex find out either. Things were hard enough as they were without involving the rest of the family. Plus Alex would more than likely deck him for the way he'd denied Patrick.

"Ah, yeah, man, anything you need, you know that."

"Thanks, man. I'll give you a call when and if I find something." Alex hung up the phone.

Jake sat in silence as he placed his phone back on the desk. What would it be like to watch as your mate's belly swelled with your child? To see them happy and content as they watched over the life growing inside them. Jake knew it would never happen for him. He had made that decision ten years ago when he had to decide what was more important, having his mate in his life or watching his mate die. He had not once, to this day, regretted the decision he'd made.

Pulling himself out of his thoughts, Jake turned the car off and got out. Looking up at the big house, he wondered what it would be like to live there and wake up every morning wrapped around the one he loved. Jake loved and hated visiting his best friend at home. Any chance he got to be in the same vicinity as his mate was both pure heaven and pure torture at the same time.

Steeling himself for the inevitable, he started up the walkway to the front door. Alex opened it before he was halfway.

"Thanks for coming, man."

"No worries. You know anytime you need anything you just have to call." Jake stopped at the door next to Alex.

"I know, come on in. Everyone else is here already." Alex slapped him on the back as he walked inside. Heading for the living room where he figured everyone would be, Jake couldn't seem to help himself, his eyes going directly to the man sitting as far away from the entry as he could get. He couldn't blame Patrick, he was in just as much pain knowing his mate was within reaching distance and not able to do anything about it.

He watched as the conversation Patrick was having with his father died. He could see Patrick taking a deep inhale of the air around him as if he could pull the air into his lungs and keep it there. Jake knew, as he was doing the same thing. Then Patrick's body tensed and he looked directly at him.

Jake watched as everything flashed across his face—hurt, longing, want, and the confusion. As much as Jake wanted to cross the room, pull his mate up into his arms, and devour his lips, he couldn't risk it. He would not put his mate in danger. Breaking the connection to Patrick, Jake made his way to the only empty seat, saying hello to everyone as he sat down.

"Jake, honey, how have you been?" Jake watched as Maryanne Holland sat playing with her new granddaughter. He knew how much she had always wanted grandcubs to spoil. Now it seemed she would be getting another one. Jake couldn't help but smile at the thought of how happy Maryanne was. He could see it in her face, her smile was wide and her eyes sparkled.

"I'm good, Mrs H. How about you?" Jake had been told more times than he could count over his life to call her Maryanne, but he just couldn't bring himself to do it when he was causing a member of their family so much pain.

Maryanne frowned slightly and looked at him. Jake smiled and shrugged his shoulders as if to say—yeah, I know, but I'm not going to change. "How could I not be good? Look how precious this little girl is, and now Marcus and Brian will be having one as well."

Jake looked at the couple in question. Marcus was settled on the couch to his right with Brian curled up in his lap. The poor man still looked pale. Marcus was gently rubbing Brian's stomach while kissing the back of his neck.

Alex cleared his throat and everyone's attention transferred to him. "Thank you all for taking time out of your Sunday to be here. I was finally able to get in contact with the Pennaeth Alpha, a man by the name of Benjamin Taylor. We were able to have a brief conversation about what is happening. Alpha Taylor informed me that he has the information that we need and has invited two members of the pack to visit and discuss this."

Alex looked at Jake and he knew what he was going to say before it left his mouth. "I am unable to get away at the moment as I am fully booked at work. Jake, as my Beta, could you go in my place?"

"Yeah, no worries, man. I don't have any pressing cases at the moment and can take a week off. When do you want me to go?"

Alex ignored his question for a minute as he turned to look at his youngest brother. Jake had a bad feeling he knew what was about to be said again and wished he could take back his agreement.

"Rick, would you consider accompanying Jake? I'm hoping that between the two of you, you can get all the information that we need in regards to Brian's condition." Patrick looked at his brothers, obviously hoping that someone else could make the trip in his place. Jake knew that wasn't possible, Alex was busy at work as he just said, there was no way in hell that Marcus was going to leave Brian behind in his condition, and Simon was newly mated and also wouldn't leave without Zack and Hayley.

Jake watched as the realisation hit Patrick and he swore before he answered his brother. "If you really think I'm needed, of course I'll go, anything for Brian."

"Thank you, both of you. I was able to get a small amount of information from Alpha Taylor over the phone." Jake watched as Alex turned all his attention to the expecting couple. "It seems that the pregnancy length you can expect is double that of a true wolf, but more than half of a regular human pregnancy. I believe this to be similar to yours, mum?"

"That sounds about right. Eighteen weeks in total, do you have any idea how far along you could be?" Maryanne asked.

Jake watched as both Brian and Marcus turned an incredible shade of red before both shook their heads.

"That's all right. Alpha Taylor has a doctor as a member of his pack who would be willing to accompany Jake and Rick home to complete a check up of Brian. He will also come out when the baby is due and help with the delivery, seeing as we can't really take you to a hospital."

"Where exactly are we going?" Patrick asked

"Cairns—well, Atherton to be exact—the town borders the state forest. The pack is apparently spread over the entire Atherton tablelands and is one of the largest in Australia."

Jake had never been to Queensland before and would be looking forward to the trip under any other circumstances; this trip however, was going to be nothing but torture. He had managed the last ten years by only allowing himself to see Patrick occasionally. Either on the night of the full moon when the entire pack got together or the odd dinner Alex invited him to. Now he was expected to be in a car and on a plane for several hours with his mate, not to mention seeing him on a daily basis for at least the next week. Yep, this trip was going to be agony.

Resigned to his fate, Jake tried to slow his racing heart. "So when do we head out?" he asked his friend.

"Well, if the pair of you can organise things tomorrow to take the time off, I will book the flights for

Tuesday and let Alpha Taylor know that you're coming." Jake nodded to show his agreement, but inside his heart was once again beating a mile a minute. One day. He had one day to get used to the idea of spending at least the next week in his mate's company and he couldn't do anything about it. Shit, he hoped his father didn't hear about this trip, at least not before he left. With that thought firmly entrenched in his mind, Jake stood.

"If you'll excuse me, I have some things to organise before we leave. Alex, if you could let me know the details as soon as you make the bookings that would be great."

"Hey man, no need to rush off. Stay for dinner. Mum's cooking tonight," Alex said, pointing back to the chair Jake had just left. He shook his head.

"Sorry, but I need to go. I have a few appointments I'll need to reschedule and some paperwork to finalise." Jake knew he was full of shit. His secretary would take care of his appointments and he never left the office on a Friday without finishing all his paperwork, but he needed to get away. He couldn't sit there and look at Patrick any longer.

Alex nodded his acceptance and Jake said goodbye to everyone, not meeting Patrick's eyes as he turned and walked away. He made it all the way outside and was almost to his car before he heard his name being called.

"Hey Jake, wait up. Please?" Jake stopped but didn't turn around. His hands curled into fists at his side to try and stop him from reaching out and grabbing hold of his mate.

"What do you want, Patrick?" Everyone else called him Rick but he'd always be Patrick to him.

"I'm sorry. He's my brother and I couldn't say no." His voice sounded so defeated that Jake spun around to stare at him. His beautiful mate stood there with his hands shoved as far into his jeans pockets as they would go, his shoulders slumped and his head forward.

Jake couldn't help himself, he reached forward and gently cupped Patrick's cheek in his large hand. "I know. It's not your fault," he whispered.

Jake stood there for a minute completely mesmerised by the emotions running through those stunning brown eyes. He felt his thumb gently caress the soft skin beneath its pad. His brain snapped back into gear and he snatched his hand away before turning and getting into his car.

His dick was now rock hard, his body yearning for that of its mate. Jake started the car and peeled away from the curb before he did anything more to put the one he loved with all his heart in any more danger.

* * * *

Rick watched as his mate once again walked away from him, well, this time he was just shy of running. He lifted his hand to his cheek, the skin still tingled from where Jake had caressed him. Sighing loudly, Rick turned and walked back into the house to join the rest of his family.

He wished he knew why Jake refused him as a mate. Was it because he wasn't gay? Maybe he just didn't find him attractive at all, or didn't want to get involved with his best friend's younger brother. Rick had longed for a reason for the last ten years, but all Jake had said was they could never be together.

That, of course, didn't stop Rick from wanting his mate. The small glimpses of Jake's body he had seen over the years at the pack gatherings fuelled his private time. His wolf didn't understand why its mate had rejected it and Rick was forced to keep a tight rein on it so he didn't shift and claim what was his whenever they were in the same room together.

Walking into the house, Rick couldn't stand the thought of going back into the lounge room with all the happy couples. Especially as he knew that would never be him. He knew who his mate was and they would never have the chance to sit cuddled up on a lazy Sunday afternoon watching football. Or get caught making out by his brothers when they came home from work.

Rick made his way to the kitchen. He wanted a drink and needed some peace so he could think. Grabbing a beer from the fridge, Rick headed outside and sat on the back steps leading from the porch to the garden. A cool breeze blew his hair and he lifted the bottle to his lips. Drinking half the beer in one go, Rick agonised over what he was going to do.

Should he find someone else and try to be happy? Even as much as Jake had hurt him over the last ten years he knew, without a doubt, he would never love another man. The thought of letting someone who wasn't Jake touch him sent shivers of revulsion down his spine. Well, it looked like his life was shaping up to be a lonely one.

Rick was so lost in his thoughts he didn't hear the back door open and was startled when Brian came and sat down beside him holding a glass of water.

"Hey," Brian said quietly.

"Hey, yourself."

"For what it's worth, I'm sorry," Brian said quietly. Confused, Rick looked at his brother-in-law.

"What in the world do you have to be sorry about?"

Brian smiled slightly at him then lowered his voice further, "I'm sorry Alex is making you go on this trip with your mate."

Rick sucked in his breath and jumped back, never once taking his eyes off the man next to him. His heart was hammering away in his chest. How did he know? Rick hadn't told a soul and he didn't think Jake would have either, seeing how he didn't want him.

Thinking fast, Rick did the only thing he could think of. He wasn't strong enough to outright deny the truth so he did the next best thing. "I don't know what you're talking about. Are you feeling okay?"

"I'm fine and you know exactly what I'm talking about. I don't know why he hasn't claimed you but I'm willing to bet everything I own that Jake is your mate."

Rick couldn't talk, his throat was burning and his head was shaking, trying to deny that which he couldn't voice. Brian placed a hand on his arm.

"It's okay, you know, to talk about it. I'm here if you ever need me."

"How—" Rick wasn't sure how he'd managed to squeeze the word out of his throat but he had and he really wanted to know how Brian had known.

"It's fairly obvious if you know what you're looking at. I noticed it the first time I met Jake. The sexual tension practically explodes around the pair of you whenever you're in the same room together. You also can't keep your eyes off him. It's almost like he can tell the exact moment you look away because then his eyes are all over you. Jason noticed it as well but your brothers seem to be particularly oblivious to the tension between you two."

Rick could feel a tear running down his cheek as he listened to Brian.

"How long have you known he was your mate?"

Rick hung his head and answered as a sob tore through him, "Ten years."

"Jesus Christ, you must have the restraint of a saint! Marcus and I couldn't even last a night after we met. Ten years—" Brian repeated. Rick didn't know if Brian sounded awed at the length of time or saddened by it.

"What are you going to do?" Brian asked him quietly.

Rick didn't know why he was opening up to Brian after he had managed to go ten years without discussing this with anyone else. Why now? "There's nothing much I can do. My mate doesn't want me and I can't stand for anyone else to touch me. Believe me, I've tried." With Jake being around so much lately and always staying as far away from Rick as he could without being rude, Rick had snapped.

"Is that where you were going in the evenings?" Rick had decided that if his mate didn't want him, he would find someone who did. So he hit the clubs and tried to pick up men. The first time Rick had almost thrown up when another man touched him. He decided he needed some liquid courage to go through with his plan. The problem with being a werewolf though, was it took a hell of a lot of alcohol to get drunk. And he meant a hell of a lot too. By the time he was starting to feel a slight buzz, the bars would be closing and he just ended up going home alone.

"Yeah, but I couldn't go through with it and all I ended up doing was drinking far too much each night. I sort of gave up about a week ago." Rick picked up his now empty beer bottle and stood. He had opened up enough for one day. Now he just wanted to be alone with his thoughts. Heading for the back door, Rick was stopped by Brian's quiet voice.

"Don't give up hope yet, Rick. I believe everything will work out in the end." Rick didn't answer. He'd had ten years of hoping his mate would come around and tell him he was madly in love with him then claim him so they could live happily ever after. If it hadn't happened so far, it wasn't going to happen. He wasn't going to say that to Brian though. He would let the man continue to think there was a happy ending to his story.

Walking inside, Rick threw his bottle in the recycling and made his way to his room, luckily avoiding everyone else in the house. He had a bag to pack and things to organise before he spent the next tortuous week in his mate's company.

CHAPTER 2

Jake couldn't believe how difficult he found it to concentrate on driving. Alex had made all the bookings and they were flying out of Albury to Sydney and then on to Cairns. They had a total of just over four hours flying time. However, they also had to get to Albury and that involved being stuck in a car with the man of his dreams for a couple of hours as well. They were due to depart Albury this afternoon at ten to five so Jake had picked Patrick up at midday to make sure they had plenty of time to reach the airport.

They were being met at Cairns airport tonight by the Beta of the Atherton pack. Right now Jake wished he was already there as being confined in this car with his mate was pure hell. Looking over once again to the man beside him, Jake was stunned at how gorgeous Patrick had grown up to be. He was sexy as sin when he was sixteen and had continued to grow into his looks as he got older.

Patrick was currently pretending to sleep with earphones in his ears, listening to his iPhone. Jake knew he was only pretending to sleep, as he could see the tension in Patrick's muscles and could hear his breathing even over the music from both the iPhone and the stereo he was currently listening to.

Patrick had said goodbye to his family and said hello to him and those had been the only words out of his mouth in the last hour. He couldn't blame his mate, as much as he would like to. Jake knew the last ten years had been hard on Patrick, especially since he didn't understand why they couldn't be together.

Jake would like nothing better than to stop the car and pull his mate into his arms and ravish his sexy mouth. He also knew that was just a dream and would never happen as long as his father lived. Jake hated his father, had for the last ten years. To think he had once looked up to the man that had sired him.

Ten years ago that had all changed. Jake had never known his father was a homophobic bastard. He had never said a word when his best friend Alex had come out of the closet. Apparently dear old dad was perfectly fine with other people being gay as long as it wasn't his son perverting himself by sleeping with men.

Jake clenched his hands around the steering wheel until his knuckles turned white. He would never forgive his father for what he had done. He may have stopped Jake from mating with Patrick but Jake refused any of the women his father had tried to set him up with over the years. He flat out refused to dishonour his mate that way.

Looking back over at his mate, Jake noticed how Patrick's hair had fallen across his face and was hiding his beautiful eyes, even if they were closed. Jake's hand twitched around the leather steering wheel, wanting nothing more than to reach out and gently tuck the runaway hair behind his sexy ear. Jake shook his head at that thought and let out a bark of laughter. Sexy ear? He really must have it bad if he found ears sexy.

Patrick seemed to give up on his attempted sleep and turned to face Jake with one eyebrow raised in question. "Sorry, just thought of something funny." Jake shrugged his shoulders not really sure what Patrick wanted him to say.

"Glad I could amuse you." The sarcasm was not lost on Jake.

"Patrick—" Jake didn't get any further before he was interrupted

"Just forget it, Jake. I don't like this situation any more than you do, but I refuse not to do everything I can to help my brother and his mate." Jake heard, loud and clear, the emphasis Patrick put on the word *mate*. Jake sighed and let the conversation drop. Nothing he said would make this situation any better so he resigned himself to saying nothing at all.

A half hour later, Jake checked the time as he felt his stomach start to rebel from not being fed recently. He had been too nervous about the trip to eat breakfast and thought they could stop on the way for lunch somewhere. Now it was nearing two in the afternoon and he had still yet to eat. Not good for a werewolf as they had a much higher metabolism than a normal human and tended to burn calories quickly. That's why there would never be an overweight werewolf. Their bodies simply burned the fat too fast.

Pulling into the next service station they came across, Jake decided he may as well refuel while he was here. "Would you like anything from inside?"

"I'll get it myself, thanks. I'm more than capable." Jake just sighed and got out of the car without replying. Grabbing the fuel nozzle, he jammed it in the tank and let it do its thing. Jake closed his eyes and rested his head against the top of the car as he held the pump. He hoped the whole week wasn't going to be like this. Was it too much to ask that his mate might actually still want him even after all this time? Jake knew the answer was more than likely—yes, it *was* too much to ask.

As the nozzle clicked off, signifying the tank was

full, Jake shook it to get every last drop of petrol out of it he could. With the way prices were going he wanted every little bit he was paying for. Walking into the shop he headed first for the drinks where he grabbed an iced coffee and then turned his attention to the food. Picking up three pies and a couple of sauces he went to pay.

Getting back into the car, Jake pulled away from the pumps and parked the car farther up towards the exit back on to the main road. Picking up his drink, he gave it a quick shake before opening the carton and downing half the milk drink in one go then picked up his first pie.

"Hungry, are we?" came an amused voice from beside him. Jake looked over and noticed Patrick was halfway through a ham and cheese sandwich and didn't seem to have anything else waiting for him.

Blushing, he nodded as he took his first bite of pie. Swallowing quickly he was glad it wasn't hot enough to burn his mouth. "Yeah. Sorry, didn't really eat this morning." Jake didn't look up, just went back to eating his late lunch.

"You know that's not good for you, right?" Did Jake detect a hint of concern in Patrick's voice? Surely not.

"Yeah, I know. Don't worry, it doesn't happen too often. I was just nervous this morning and couldn't eat."

Jake winced as soon as he realised what he'd said. Why on earth would he have told Patrick that? The only feasible explanation he could come up with was prolonged exposure to Patrick was turning his brain to mush. He just hoped that Patrick would ignore it and finish his sandwich.

No such luck, however. "Why were you too nervous to eat?" Patrick asked quietly, never lifting his gaze from the food held in his hand.

Jake finished his pie and grabbed the next one. Opening the package it was in he shrugged and answered, "It doesn't matter. Forget I said anything."

Patrick tightened his hold on his food and clenched his teeth. "Tell me!"

"Fine! I was nervous about seeing you. I am every time I visit your house. But being with you nonstop for at least the next week and not being able to touch you is killing me inside." Jake grabbed his food and left the car, slamming the door behind him. He knew he shouldn't have said it but he just couldn't seem to stop the words from flowing out of his mouth.

Walking over to the sole picnic table next to the servo, Jake sat on the table with his feet on the concrete seat. Burying his head in his hands, he wondered just how he was going to survive the next week.

* * * *

"What the hell does that mean?" Rick asked the empty car as he was left alone while Jake once again walked away from him. He was getting pretty sick and tired of watching his mate's back as he left. Running Jake's words over again in his head he wondered if they really meant what he thought they did. Could Jake really want him? If so, then what in the hell was keeping them apart?

Rick sat and watched Jake while he tried to finish the food he had bought. The sandwich, however, tasted like ash in his mouth so he packed it away to throw in the bin. Rick continued to watch his mate for the next half hour while Jake ate his third pie and looked up at the sky. He seemed to heave a big sigh, then stood and threw his rubbish away before making his way back to the car.

Jake got back in the car and started the engine. Not a word was spoken as he pulled back on to the road and headed to Albury. Rick was about to open his mouth to ask what exactly Jake had meant by his earlier comments when Jake beat him to it.

"Don't Patrick, please. It's doesn't matter." Jake sounded so defeated Rick was hard pressed not to reach out to him.

"It does matter, Jay, don't you see that?" Jake visibly winced then shook his head at the nickname Rick had given him when he was a kid.

Jake didn't reply though. He just sat there and concentrated on driving. Rick sighed and turned to stare out the window at the passing trees. Within, his wolf was howling, longing for his mate, knowing he was so close. Squeezing his eyes shut tight he refused to let the tears, which were desperately trying to escape, fall.

Less than a half hour later they finally pulled up at the Albury Airport. Jake parked the car and they grabbed their bags and made their way inside. Rick was glad to be out of the car. The scent of Jake seemed to have taken up residence in his nose and didn't want to leave. He hoped to Christ the airport would change that fact. Jake's rich scent was driving him insane.

They waited in line until they were called then checked in. Making their way to the boarding lounge, Rick got himself a bottle of water from one of the airport kiosks. Sitting down to wait, he pulled out his Kindle and settled down to read. If he happened to be ignoring his stubborn mate at the same time, all the better.

A nudge to his arm pulled his attention back to the

airport. "What?"

"It's time to board." Rick was startled by this.

"Really?"

"Yes, you've had your head in that thing for nearly an hour." Rick smiled to himself. It sounded like Jake was a little annoyed at him. Oh well.

Grabbing his carry case and his boarding pass, Rick stood and made his way to the entrance. Once they were seated on the plane Rick tried to make himself comfortable again. This however proved to be a hard task as their first plane was only a Qantas link flight and has nothing but economy seating. This, for two very large werewolves, made for a tight fit. Thank god the flight only lasted for an hour and Alex had booked them in business class from Sydney to Cairns.

Rick made sure to turn the wi-fi in his Kindle off so he could read while they were flying. Once the aircraft had taken off and levelled out, he faced towards the window and started reading again. Jake sat beside him typing away on his laptop. The steady click of the keys soothed something deep down inside Rick that he didn't want to examine too closely.

They were soon asked to pack away all electronics for the landing in Sydney. Once they had touched down and departed the plane they made their way through the very large and very busy Sydney airport to their next departure gate. They had an hour and a half wait until their next flight was due to depart.

By mutual agreement they ate a quick dinner at one of the restaurants in the airport, even though they would be served food on their next flight. The meal was a quiet affair with neither of them knowing what to say to the other without bringing up the huge pink elephant in the room.

Soon after finishing their meal, their flight was called for boarding. Jake paid the check and they made their way to the boarding gate once again. Rick sighed with happiness when he sat down in business class. Jake laughed behind him and stowed their hand luggage in the overhead lockers. Rick looked at him and raised an eyebrow in question.

Jake just shook his head and continued to smile. He sat in the seat next to him and handed over Rick's Kindle. "Thought you might want this for the flight."

"Thank you." Rick placed his Kindle in the seat pocket in front of him and stretched his legs out. It felt so good to have room to move.

They waited on the tarmac for nearly twenty minutes while everyone else took their seats and they were given permission to take off. An hour into the flight, after the food had been served and cleared away, Rick turned his overhead light off and curled onto his side, facing the window, to get some sleep before landing. Today had been one of the hardest days he'd had in years. He was emotionally exhausted and needed some time to recharge his batteries.

With the scent of his mate so close to him, he settled down easily and drifted off to sleep.

CHAPTER 3

Jake looked down at his mate who was currently curled into his side, holding on to his arm as if he'd never let go. He knew he shouldn't have lifted the arm rest between them but he couldn't help it. Not long after Patrick had gone to sleep, he had rolled over and cuddled close to Jake's side. His head was currently resting against Jake's shoulder with both hands wrapped around his left arm, holding it tightly.

Lifting his right hand, Jake did what he'd wanted to do all day and gently tucked Patrick's runaway hair behind his ear. Not being able to stop himself, he leant forward and placed a gentle kiss on his mate's forehead. "I love you, Patrick," he whispered. The first time he'd ever told his mate how he felt, and he wasn't awake to hear the words.

Jake watched as Patrick smiled and sighed contentedly in his sleep before snuggling in even closer. Having his mate so close had calmed the constant restlessness of his wolf, who was currently curled up is a ball happily sleeping inside him.

He wished he could sleep as easily as his wolf, but Jake knew he couldn't pass up the opportunity to watch his mate while he slumbered.

The flight seemed to pass entirely too quickly for Jake's liking; the captain came over the speakers requesting the cabin crew prepare the aircraft for landing. Sighing at the thought of waking Patrick and once more seeing the walls go up around him, Jake bent down and gently kissed his mate for what was probably the last time.

Sitting back Jake gently cupped Patrick's cheek before softly calling his name. It took a couple of tries but Patrick's eyes eventually fluttered open. Man, he was sexy when he was all sleep-tousled and confused. Jake watched as Patrick blinked a couple of times then recognition swept back into his body and Patrick jerked away.

Jake hid the pain that action caused him, but understood why Patrick had done it.

"Umm—" Even his voice was sexy as hell when he just woke up. Jake was having a hard time keeping the smile from his face. "Sorry for falling asleep on you. It won't happen again." Jake watched as pink suffused Patrick's cheeks and he refused to look at Jake.

"It's no problem. You can fall asleep on me anytime you want." Shit! Now why in the hell did he go and say that? Nothing like waving a red flag in front of a bull, now was there?

Patrick jerked around and stared at him, his eyes

narrowed as he glared at Jake, obviously trying to figure out if he was joking or not. "Yeah, right. I'll keep that in mind," Patrick ground out through clenched teeth before jamming the armrest down between them and buckling his seatbelt. He then turned to stare out the window and completely ignored Jake for the short time they had left on the flight.

* * * *

Rick was furious with himself. He hadn't meant to fall asleep on Jake, but he had to admit to himself it was the best sleep he'd had in a long time. Even if it was only for a couple of hours. He hated Jake for making a joke about him falling asleep on him. It obviously didn't matter to the other man that they were fated mates and were meant to be together. Shit! If the last ten years didn't tell him the same thing then Rick didn't know what would.

Standing and grabbing his bag from the overhead locker when the plane had come to a stop, Rick stared at the man in front of him. Jake stood four inches over six feet and had hair as black as the night, with eyes as blue as the pacific that melted Rick's heart each and every time he looked at them. At the moment he was staring at the back of Jake's neck and could see what he thought was the tip of a tattoo reaching up from under the collar of his shirt.

Rick was curious as to what his mate had hidden under his shirt. He wasn't aware Jake had any tattoos, but then again there was a lot he didn't know about Jake. Jake turned side on as if he could feel Rick's eyes boring into his neck. This gave Rick the perfect opportunity to look into the face of the man he loved. The permanent three day growth covering Jake's cheeks was neatly trimmed.

He couldn't believe how sexy Jake looked with the stubble on his cheeks. Rick had never once even looked at a clean shaven man in the last ten years, they did nothing for him. He liked the feel of the rough hair under his fingers. Not that he had gotten the opportunity to feel Jake's skin and hair under his fingers very often.

Rick's thoughts were interrupted by a rough shove from behind him. Stumbling forward he realised Jake no longer stood there and the rest of the passengers were waiting on him to move so they could all depart. Jake was waiting for him on the other side of the airplane door with a curious expression of his face.

Deciding to ignore the unasked question Rick followed behind Jake as they made their way down the corridor and into the main airport. They travelled down the escalator to the ground floor where the baggage claim was. They weren't exactly sure how long they were going to be here so they'd both packed a small suitcase with enough clothes for a week away.

Stepping off the escalator Rick noticed a tall man holding a sign with their names—Holland and Richmond—on it. He nudged Jake and pointed in the man's direction. They changed their course and headed towards the man with the sign.

Once they arrived the tall, sexy man held his hand out for Jake. "Liam Anderson, Beta of the Atherton pack. Welcome to Cairns."

Jake shook his hand. "Jake Richmond, Beta of the Leyburn pack. Thank you for having us. This here is Patrick Holland, brother to the Alpha."

Liam nodded in understanding, and then raked his eyes up and down the entire length of Rick's body before he held his hand out in greeting. "Nice to meet you, Patrick." Liam's voice had dropped several octaves lower.

Rick shook hands with the hot Beta then tipped his head to the side in submission to the stronger wolf. If the other man held his hand slightly longer than necessary, Rick wasn't going to say anything. "Nice to meet you too. Please call me Rick, everyone does." Rick heard the low growl coming from the man standing beside him.

Turning to glare at the angry wolf, he raised an eyebrow. "And what's your problem?"

"Nothing," Jake bit out through clenched teeth before turning and heading to collect their bags.

"Sorry, didn't mean to step on any toes," Liam said laughing, as he stood beside Rick and they watched Jake stalk through the airport.

"Don't worry, you didn't. Jake doesn't want me," Rick said quietly.

"Good. That means you're available," Liam said with a broad smile that lit up hit face.

Rick blushed. "We'll see," he said then turned back to Jake who had returned with their bags.

"Let's go," Jake grunted out. They followed Liam as he led them out of the terminal and into the car park, stopping at a dark Mitsubishi. It was hard to tell the exact colour of the car due to the lateness of the hour. Liam stowed their bags in the boot.

"Now, do either of you get car sick?" he asked.

"Not that I know of, why?" Jake asked.

Liam just grinned at them. "You'll see."

Jake opened the rear door and waited for Rick to get in. He raised his eyebrow in question but didn't get a reply.

Sighing in resignation Rick got in the car, he wasn't expecting Jake to get in behind him though. Sliding over, he found himself sitting behind the front passenger seat with Jake seated behind Liam.

It was fairly obvious that Jake didn't want Rick sitting in the front, too close to Liam. What he didn't understand was why. Jake had made it clear as day he wasn't wanted, so why did he care if someone else wanted Rick.

Thinking he would never understand his mate, Rick sat back and watched the scenery as they left the airport and drove through the outer suburbs of Cairns. After about twenty minutes Liam looked over his shoulder at him.

"Are you ready for this?"

"Are we ready for what exactly?" Rick replied, suspicious now.

"The Gillies," Liam answered with a chuckle. As it turned out, the Gillies was a stretch of road nearly twenty kilometres long that wound up and down the side of the mountains. It had two hundred sixty-three turns in that short distance and rose up eight hundred meters.

Rick felt every one of the turns, and by the time they came down the other side to smooth straight road again he was feeling decidedly green around the gills, which was an entirely new experience for him. Jake on the other hand looked fine. Bastard!

Another twenty minutes later and they reached Atherton. "I'm not sure if anyone informed you but you will be staying at my house for the duration of your stay." Jake growled beside him and Rick lightly slapped his arm.

"Cut it out." Jake just ignored him and continued to growl quietly. They soon pulled into the driveway of a standard looking house.

"It's not much, but it's home. Let's get your things and get you settled," Liam said as he shut off the car then got out.

After the front door had been closed, Rick shot his hand out to hold Jake back for a minute. "Just what exactly is your problem?"

"I don't like him," Jake answered shortly.

"Why the hell not? He seems nice to me."

"That's why I don't like him." And with that answer Jake pulled his arm away from Rick's grip and got out of the car.

Rick shook his head. God, that man drove him crazy. If he didn't know better he would think that Jake was jealous, but that couldn't be right, could it? Deciding to ignore that question for the time being, Rick exited the car and walked around the back to grab his luggage before following Liam up the short path to the front door.

The interior of the house was decorated much like a typical bachelor pad—dark colours, large flat screen TV, leather couches. There were a couple of pieces of artwork hanging on the walls and a few photos scattered around the place. Liam led them down a hallway and pointed out where Jake and he would be sleeping.

Once Rick had put his luggage in his room, Liam showed him where the bathroom, toilet and kitchen were.

Trying to ignore the heat coming off Jake's body right behind him he took a step forward, which unfortunately put him closer to Liam and started Jake with the low growling again.

"On that note, I think I'm going to shower and go to bed. It's been a hell of a long day." Rick turned and had to push his way past Jake to exit the kitchen where they had ended the tour.

Going to his room, Rick unzipped his suitcase and found his shaving kit. He grabbed the clean towel from the foot of the bed and made his way to the bathroom. Rick turned the water on to heat up as he quickly divested himself of his clothes. Picking up the items from his kit that he needed, he stepped under the now warm water.

As he stood there, hands against the tiled wall, letting the water rain down on his head, Rick felt himself relaxing for possibly the first time today, except maybe his nap on the plane. He allowed the water to carry away the tension in his muscles and the ache in his gut. After several minutes of standing still and enjoying the water Rick thought he better finish up. Quickly shampooing his hair and washing his body, Rick stepped out of the shower five minutes later.

He dried himself off then wrapped the towel around his waist as he picked up his clothes and shaving kit and headed back to his room. As luck would have it, as soon as he stepped out of the bathroom, Jake turned down the hall. They stood frozen in place staring at each other until Jake ripped his eyes away from him and walked into his bedroom, slamming the door behind him.

"Well, tell me how you really feel," Rick mumbled under his breath as he made his way into his own room. Placing his clothes next to his suitcase Rick hung his towel on the hook on the back of the door, before crawling into bed. Slipping between the fresh, clean, warm sheets Rick felt his body relax as he slowly drifted off to sleep.

CHAPTER 4

Jake stood in the kitchen with the Atherton Beta and watched as Patrick practically ran from the room. Turning his attention back to the man currently leaning against one of the kitchen benches, Jake bared his teeth and growled again.

"Stay away from Patrick," he bit out between clenched teeth. Liam just smiled at him.

"Why the hell should I? He's cute and available." Liam shoved his hands in the front pockets of his jeans, bringing Jake's eyes down to the substantial bulge hidden within. Tearing his gaze back up to the grinning Beta, Jake growled again. He seemed to be doing a lot of that since they had landed.

"He's not available." Jake knew it was the wrong thing to say as soon as the words left his mouth but he couldn't seem to bite them back. Liam just continued to look at him questioningly.

"Really? 'Cause according to the man in question, he's available."

"Well, he's not. So keep your dick in your pants while we're here." With that Jake stalked from the kitchen and headed off to his room. Before he could reach the safety of his room, the most beautiful vision stepped out of the bathroom amidst a cloud of steam.

Jake had to swallow hard in order to stop himself from telling the vision in front of him exactly what he thought. Patrick stood still, his chest bare and still slightly damp from his shower, his golden skin gleamed in the low light of the passage. Jake raked his eyes down the soft treasure trail of light brown hair that led from his belly button down below a towel that had been wrapped precariously around his waist.

He took an involuntary step forward, then realised what he had done and ripped his eyes away from his mate and took shelter in his room. Jake leant back against the door causing it to slam shut behind him. His chest was heaving, his cock was rock hard and pushing against the confines of his pants.

Ripping his button open and tugging his fly down, Jake's hand dove into his underwear and pulled out his aching length, pumping it furiously. Images of his nearly naked mate played through his mind as if they were on slow motion replay. A half dozen more strokes and Jake howled as his orgasm slammed into him and his cock erupted with pearly white strings of cum all over his chest and hand.

Jake's legs gave out and he collapsed on to the floor beneath him, back still pressed hard against the door. How the hell was he supposed to last a week in his mate's company if one look at the man sent this kind of reaction through his body? Who was he kidding? He would be lucky if he lasted another day.

* * * *

Liam smiled as he watched the Leyburn Beta stalk from the room. He had known the two men were mates the second he'd met them. It was a gift he had been born with. He could see the mating threads of his kind and could recognise a destined couple immediately upon meeting both parties. He didn't know why Jake and Rick had yet to complete their bond but he intended to do everything possible to rectify the situation.

If he just happened to annoy the other Beta along the way with his supposed interest in Rick, then all the better. It certainly looked to be an interesting week.

* * * *

Jake had never had a worse night's sleep in his

entire life. After all the tension of their travel yesterday and his explosive orgasm last night, he had expected to drift right off to sleep. Instead he lay there in a foreign bed staring at the ceiling all night. His mate's faint scent was drifting into his room from next door. Jake had jerked off twice more during the night in the hope he would finally relax enough to get some sleep.

Giving up on getting any decent amount of sleep at five thirty, Jake decided to go for a run and see the town. Slipping out of bed he used the bathroom before searching in his suitcase for his running gear. Once he was dressed in his old footy shorts and tank top, he tied his sneakers and quietly left the house. Just because he couldn't sleep, didn't mean the others couldn't.

Jake locked the door behind him. He stood in the middle of the front yard and did his warm up stretches as a cold breeze blew through. The cold didn't affect werewolves as much as it did humans as they ran at a higher body temperature.

Finishing his stretches Jake took off out of the yard and down the road. He had no idea where he was going, he just knew he had to get away for a while. Breathing in the crisp clean air of the nearby forest was exhilarating and caused his wolf to stir within, wanting out to be able to run as well. The full moon was in two nights and they would be spending it here with the Atherton pack.

Jake turned down several side streets before he finally came to what looked to be the main road through the town. He glanced at the stores along the path as he ran past, not really paying much attention to what they held within. He followed the road the entire way until the town seemed to end and giant fields of sugarcane took over.

The sun was just rising in the east over the field and the sight was spectacular. Jake paused in his run and just stood there watching the sky turn from a dark grey to a dusty pink then a light blue. Patrick would love this view. Jake tried to nip that thought in the bud, but knew he was correct. Patrick never left home without a camera when he was younger and would have loved the sight of the sun rising over the sugarcane.

Jake sighed. Even when trying to clear his head and forget about the fact that his mate was so close, it seemed Patrick was never far from his thoughts. That's the way it'd been for the last ten years and Jake didn't see it changing anytime soon, no matter how much he wished it would sometimes.

Starting his jog home again before his muscles cramped from his prolonged stop, Jake took several more back roads to continue his exploration. It was just after seven when Jake finally made it back to Liam's house. He once again stopped on the lawn and stretched his now aching leg muscles to prevent any cramping.

After ten minutes of stretching Jake looked up and noticed Patrick standing in the living room peeking out from beside the curtain. As soon as Patrick noticed Jake looking at him, he snatched his hand away and the curtain fluttered closed once again. Deciding to ignore it as it was too early in the morning to start in on Patrick, Jake made his way up the walk and to the front door. Grabbing the handle and turning it as he continued to walk forward, Jake was expecting the door to open. Instead it remained stubbornly closed, causing him to walk face first into the solid wooden door.

Jake cursed as he grabbed for his nose, the instant flare of pain bringing tears to his eyes. Pulling his hand away he was thankful there wasn't any blood. Cursing again Jake pounded on the door. It flew open seconds later with Patrick standing on the other side, his hand covering his mouth, obviously trying to hide his amusement. His eyes said it all though, they lit up with suppressed mirth. Happiness looked good on Patrick.

"Not a single word," Jake growled.

"I didn't say a thing," Patrick replied, humour evident in his voice. Jake made it all the way to the hall before he heard the laughter bubbling up from behind him. He couldn't help but smile, his mate was happy at the moment so who was he to argue with that even if he looked like an idiot.

Grabbing his shaving kit, Jake made his way into the bathroom to shower the sweat from his body.

Once he had finished Jake grabbed the towel he had placed on the toilet lid and dried off. He pulled on a pair of boxer briefs then wrapped the towel around his waist. Standing in front of the mirror, Jake rested his hands on either side of the sink and just stared at his reflection for a while. His coal-black hair, still damp from the shower, looked as if he'd run his hands through it constantly. His blue eyes stared back at him, as deep and as troubled as some of the stormiest seas.

Jake lifted one hand and rubbed it across his stubbled cheek. He knew that Patrick liked him with stubble. It was something that had been said over ten years ago but Jake didn't care. If Patrick liked it, he would do whatever he could to make the man even the slightest bit happy. Seriously, growing a little facial hair was nothing, so Jake maintained his look even if he only saw his mate once a month at the pack gatherings on the full moon.

The very edges of the tattoo that had graced his back for so many years caught his eyes. The tattoo was a constant reminder of what he was supposed to have and had given up. He had kept it hidden from everyone, making sure no one ever stood behind him when he shifted and even going to a different town to have the work done. Even Alex, his best friend, and one of the best tattoo artists in the state, didn't know what his tattoo looked like.

Pushing away from the sink Jake took one last look before gathering his stuff and exiting from the bathroom. Careful to keep his exposed back out of view from either Patrick or Liam, Jake hurried to his room.

Dressed in a pair of black slacks and a blue button-down shirt, Jake made his way to the kitchen to find something to eat and find out the plan for the day. Walking into the room he became immediately suspicious as the conversation between Liam and Patrick cut off abruptly with his arrival. He looked at Patrick, but the man remained quiet, looking down at the toast on the plate in front of him, However, Jake did notice the pink making its way up his cheeks.

"Morning," he said gruffly as he grabbed a cup of coffee from the pot on the bench before he took a seat at the table. Taking a sip of his coffee, Jake never removed his eyes from the blushing cheeks of his mate. He wondered what the hell they had been talking about to cause such a reaction in Patrick.

Finally tearing his eyes away he turned to Liam who was currently watching him. Jake growled. Liam seemed to bring out the worst in him and Jake didn't like it. Liam laughed, there was movement under the table seconds before Jake was kicked in the shin. "Argh… shit, that hurt. Who the hell kicked me and why?" Jake leant down to rub his leg where he had been assaulted.

Liam roared with laughter and Jake growled again. He didn't see what was so funny. Looking at Patrick he noticed the pink in his cheeks had turned to full on red and he refused to meet his eyes. Jake took a deep breath to calm down. Once he knew he could talk in a reasonable voice again, he turned to Liam.

"So what's the plan for while we're here?" he asked.

Stifling his laughter, it took Liam a minute to compose himself enough to be able to answer. "As you can imagine, being the Penneath Alpha of all the packs in Australia, Ben is a very busy man. At the moment he currently has three other Alphas that were called in for emergency meetings staying with him. That is why you're with me instead of being a guest at the Alpha's house."

Jake could understand that. He didn't know how Alex handled being Alpha of their pack, let alone being the head of all the packs across Australia.

"So I'm sorry to say the meeting that had been set aside for today has been postponed, at least until tomorrow. Depending on how his meetings go today," Liam continued.

Jake nodded, he could understand there were more important things the Alpha had to deal with than their meeting, as they were only looking for information.

"So where does that leave us for the day?" Patrick finally decided to join the conversation.

"I suppose wherever you want. You can hang out here all day or you can take my truck and go for a drive and explore the area. The tablelands really are very beautiful and you have been invited to join the pack tomorrow for the full moon run." Liam paused as he looked down at his watch, "Unfortunately, I will have to leave you to it as I need to get to work. The keys to the truck are hanging over there and there is a key to the house with them." Liam pointed to a small row of hooks above one of the kitchen benches. There were several sets of keys hanging side by side.

Liam stood from the table and walked into the kitchen where he washed his coffee cup and plate before drying his hands. He grabbed one of the sets of keys from the hooks and said his goodbyes as he walked out of the kitchen. Jake soon heard the front door closing behind him.

Quiet settled over the house as it struck Jake that he had just been left alone with his mate in a very private setting. Driving and flying with Patrick, as hard as that had been, had allowed him to keep his hands to himself as they were constantly moving or in very public places. However, now they were in a house, all by themselves, with flat surfaces, and couches, and beds. Jake bit back a moan at the thought of Patrick laid out on any of the latter, all naked and wanting. Pushing back from the table so fast his chair clattered to the ground behind him, Jake stood there breathing hard as he tried to gather his resolve.

Patrick placed a hand gently on his arm. "Hey, Jay, you okay?" Jake shook his head. His skin felt like it was burning from the gentle touch of his mate. His wolf felt like a battering ram inside him, trying desperately to get to his mate. Jake groaned and gave in.

He grabbed Patrick's hand from where it rested on his arm and pulled the man from his chair until he had him settled into his arms. Wrapping one hand around the back of Patrick's neck, he held the man still as he devoured the sweetest lips in history. Patrick whimpered into his mouth before Jake felt his arms wrap around his neck. Licking Patrick's bottom lip, the man opened to him and Jake invaded his mouth as if it was the last supply of water to a dying man.

Jake's tongue tangled with that of his mate, exploring everything, teeth, gums, tongue, and lips. Patrick tasted like ambrosia, with just a hint of coffee and Jake couldn't get enough. It was the first time in ten years he had given into his feelings and kissed Patrick and the man tasted just as good now as he had the last time they kissed. And with that thought all the reasons for his staying away came crashing back. Jake moved his hands, wrapped them around Patrick's upper arms and pushed the man away.

Patrick whimpered when they broke apart and tried to step into him again, reaching for his neck to pull him back down.

"No!" Jake growled and Patrick stopped still. "That shouldn't have happened." He watched as the look of hope and happiness faded from his mate's face. Patrick's red, kiss-swollen lips turned down in a frown and the light seemed to seep out of his eyes. Jake turned and walked away. If he didn't there was no way he could have stopped himself from dragging Patrick to his room and making the man his forever. He slammed the front door behind him in his frustration.

Jake knew what he had just done had possibly killed any feelings Patrick might still have for him but there wasn't a lot he could do about that now. Running his hands through his hair he sat on one of the chairs on the front porch and buried his face in his hands. When the tears started to fall, he ignored them.

Chapter 5

Rick sat in the living room staring out the window. He watched as the day passed slowly by. Jake didn't come back inside and they didn't go exploring the tablelands together like Liam has suggested. Instead Rick sat in silence, his mind surprisingly blank as he watched the sun rise and fall. The shadows across the room lengthened and Rick thought absently that Liam should soon be back.

He hadn't eaten anything since breakfast as he didn't think he would be able to keep it down. Hearing the door close some time later and a throat clear, Rick was pulled from his staring contest with a gecko that had taken up residence on the outside of the window.

Looking up, he noticed Liam standing there with a bemused expression on his face. "Everything okay?"

"Uh huh." Rick didn't know what else to say. Should he tell Liam how lonely he had been for the last ten years? Should he tell him that he died inside today when his mate yet again rejected him? Or that he had been sitting here all day and had no idea where Jake had gone? Or maybe he should tell Liam he wanted him to take him to his room and fuck his brains out as it seemed he wasn't wanted by anyone else.

Rick couldn't get any of those things to pass his lips so he just continued to sit quietly.

"Right, well I've known you less than twenty-four hours and I can tell you're full of shit." Rick nodded his head slightly in acceptance of this fact. "Come on. I'm starved, and I know a great little pizza place."

Rick didn't feel like going out, but he didn't have much choice when Liam walked up to him and literally pulled him out of his chair. Rick chuckled as the pair collided and once he was steady on his feet, Liam turned him around and shoved him towards the door.

"You are coming with me whether you like it or not, even if I have to push you the whole way there." Rick's lips twitched, trying to smile. He turned his head to look at the man behind him and raised an eyebrow in challenge. Liam walked right up to him and shoved him in the back again.

Rick shot forward several feet farther then came to a complete stop. This happened several more times until they came to the front door. Liam opened the door then quickly shoved Rick through.

He laughed as he stumbled and nearly toppled down the path. His stumble came to an abrupt end when a large hand clamped around his arm and pulled him upright. Rick turned, expecting to see Liam behind him once again but came face to face with Jake. The laughter died in his throat and the smile vanished from his face. He ripped his arm out of Jake's hold, not wanting the man who had broken his heart, yet again, to touch him.

Rick stepped purposefully back until he was out of grabbing range before he turned and walked towards Liam's car. The locks disengaged and Rick jerked the door open and got in the front seat of the car before slamming the door behind him. Not once did he look at the man that stood still as a rock staring back at him.

Liam slid into the seat next to him and started the car. "I don't know what happened today between the two of you but could you please try not to take it out on my poor defenceless baby?"

Rick chuckled at the car being called a baby. "Yeah, sorry about that. Your baby's safe." Rick put his seatbelt on and settled back for the short ride to the restaurant. Despite what he had said earlier he was actually looking forward to going out, he would have preferred it to be with Jake but beggars couldn't be choosers.

Five minutes later they pulled up out front of a typical little pizza place. There were only a dozen tables in the small restaurant, with half of those already filled. The place seemed to do a roaring trade in take away as there were several people waiting on their orders and several more lined up to place one.

A waiter showed them to their table before handing them a menu each. Scanning the lengthy list of pizzas the place provided, Rick decided to stick with his favourite, deep pan barbeque meat lovers. Once their orders were placed and the drinks had arrived, Rick sat back and tried not to feel uncomfortable as Liam stared at him.

"What?" he growled when he couldn't handle the silence any longer.

Liam shrugged. "Nothing really, was just wondering if you were planning on telling me what happened between you and your mate today."

Rick felt like the wind was just knocked out of him, he couldn't breathe. It was bad enough he wasn't good enough for his mate, now the man sitting in front of him knew it as well. The breath he had been holding whooshed from his body and Rick felt lightheaded. It wasn't until Rick felt a palm gently cup his cheek that he realised he had been shaking his head back and forth.

"It's okay, you know," Liam said gently as he moved his hand to settle it on the table between them.

Rick shook his head once more. "No, it's not. That man is not my mate. He doesn't want me and that's all I'm going to say about it."

Liam nodded. "Fine, but I'm here if you ever want to talk."

"Thanks, do you mind if we change the subject to something a little less depressing?" Rick asked.

"Sure, how about you tell me how long I have to wait until I can get you naked?" Liam asked with a straight face. Rick's jaw dropped, then he broke out laughing as Liam waggled his eyebrows suggestively, a huge grin now covering his face.

As their laughter died down their pizza was served. The pair settled back to enjoy their meal.

* * * *

Once again Jake had one of the worst nights of his life. Patrick and Liam had returned two hours after they had left to go have pizza the previous night. Since when did it take two hours to eat a pizza? Jake had spent the quiet time pacing the living room cursing himself for a fool.

When the pair had finally walked through the door laughing and falling all over each other Jake had stood there and growled. Patrick rolled his eyes at him before throwing a pizza his way and heading down the hall to his room. Liam just shook his head before he too left him to his misery.

Jake had eaten the pizza purely for the reason that he was a werewolf and it wasn't a good idea to go an entire day without food. Once the pizza was finished it sat like a lead weight in his stomach for the remainder of the evening.

Giving up around ten that evening he went to bed. Patrick hadn't come back out of his room the rest of the night. The previous night's lack of sleep helped Jake to succumb to the darkness relatively quickly. Jake woke less than an hour later breathing heavy and finding his chest covered in his sticky seed. He'd groaned as he remembered the dream he'd been having.

Jake woke twice more like that throughout the night. Needless to say he was exhausted by the time he got out of bed the next morning. It wasn't the first time he'd had a wet dream since finding his mate. It was however the first time it had happened three times in one night.

He decided to forgo a run that morning as he just didn't have the energy. Instead, while the rest of the house was relatively quiet, Jake made his way to the bathroom. He set the water to warm up as he ran the clippers over his short beard to keep the hair at a reasonable length.

Once happy with the results, Jake stepped into the now hot shower and stayed there, not moving for several minutes, just letting the water cascade down his exhausted body. Finally moving he reached for the soap. Lathering it in his hands he scrubbed his groin and chest thoroughly, cleaning away any dried cum still left on his body. Happy he was sufficiently clean Jake turned the water off.

Drying himself, he opened the bathroom door and checked the passage before hurrying to his room. With everything that had happened the previous day he didn't want Patrick to see his back.

Once he was dressed Jake made his way to the kitchen, and noticed no one else seemed to be up yet. He made a pot of coffee and poured a cup for himself before he settled at the table to wait for Patrick and Liam to wake.

Jake was lost in thought when Liam walked through the kitchen door a half hour later. "Morning."

"Morning," Jake replied. "Is our meeting with Alpha Taylor still on for today?"

"Yes. Ben called me last night to confirm. Your meeting is set for eight-thirty this morning. As I have to work, I'll be able to drop you off but I can't pick you up when your business has been concluded. So you can borrow my truck and follow me there if you like, that way you have transport so you can leave when you need," Liam informed him.

"Sounds good." Looking at his watch he wondered if someone should go wake Patrick when the man walked through the door. He was wearing nothing but a pair of boxer shorts, his hair was sticking up all over the place and his cheek still had an indent from where he had pressed against his pillow. Personally Jake thought he'd never looked better.

He bit back yet another growl at the thought of Liam seeing so much of his mate's naked skin, but knew he had no right to be so possessive. Patrick went straight to the coffee. Once he'd taken the first couple of sips he turned to face the room. Seeing both Liam and Jake staring at him Patrick blushed to the tips of his ears. "Oops," he whispered before putting his coffee down and walking back out of the room.

Liam laughed. Jake just stared at the man now sitting across the table from him. His lips pulled into a tight line across his face. Patrick retuned ten minutes later, Jake didn't know if he was thankful or not that his mate was now dressed.

A half hour later they left and headed to the Alpha's house. Patrick didn't speak to him the entire fifteen minute trip. Pulling up beside Liam's sedan Jake parked the car and got out. "I'll show you in and introduce you to the Alpha, then, unfortunately, I have to get to work," Liam said as they walked the path leading up to the large two story house.

The place was smaller than the one Patrick shared with his brothers, but then he supposed the Penneath Alpha didn't share his house with six other fully grown men. Liam rang the bell when they stood in front of the door. The door was inlaid with three intricate glass panels. The centre one showed a large black wolf standing in a field, howling at the moon. In the background and spread over the two other panels, was his pack. Jake had never seen a more stunning piece of glass.

He was still staring at the picture when the door opened. The man in the doorway must have stood at least six foot six. He had to be late thirties with broad shoulders, short, dark brown almost black hair and piercing blue eyes. "Morning Ben." Jake heard Liam greet the man. There was no mistaking this man to be anyone but the Penneath Alpha, the power just poured off him.

"Hey Liam, come on in." The deep voice of the Alpha replied as he stepped back and allowed them entry to his house. Ben led them through the house to his office.

Once there Liam introduced them.

"Alpha Taylor, this is Jake Richmond, Beta of the Leyburn pack and Patrick Holland, brother to the pack Alpha."

Jake shook the Alpha's hand and tilted his head to the side, exposing his neck, as a sign of submission to the dominant man in front of him. Alpha Taylor gently touched his neck in acknowledgment. "Nice to meet you, Jake."

"You too, Alpha," Jake replied.

"Please, call me Ben. I don't stand on formality unless it's absolutely necessary."

"Thank you, Ben," Jake replied as Ben moved to stand in front of Patrick. When Patrick exposed his neck to the other man Jake had a hard time fighting the snarl that wanted to escape his lips. He really didn't like his mate exposing his delicate neck to anyone but him.

Ben led them to a set of leather couches that were set to the side in his large office and they all sat down. Liam said his goodbyes and headed off to work.

"Now, tell me what's happened to your pack member."

CHAPTER 6

Where to start? Rick supposed the beginning was as good as any other place. Looking at Jake he received a nod to indicate it was his story to tell. "Nine months ago my brother Marcus met his mate Brian. After a few hiccups they mated and have been happy ever since."

Ben nodded for him to continue.

"About two weeks ago Brian got ill. He can hardly keep anything down due to the constant vomiting, the smell of certain foods turns his stomach, and his skin has become very sensitive. Needless to say, we were all extremely worried.

"Last week a couple from our pack came to visit after hearing of Brian's illness. Tegan and her mate Mitchell explained how they'd come to be guardians to Mitchell's nephew. You can imagine the surprise on all of our faces when Mitchell informed us that his brother, Lucas, had given birth to the child."

Ben smiled. "Yes, I guess news like that would come as a bit of a surprise. Now, I spoke with your brother briefly last week and gave him as much information as I was comfortable giving out over the phone." Ben maintained eye contact with Rick while he spoke.

Shifting his gaze now to Jake, he continued, "I am pleased he could trust his Beta with this information in his stead."

"Thank you, Ben. Alex and I have been friends for over twenty years and I trust him with my life, as he does me. He would have been here himself if not for a very full work schedule." Rick deflated a little at that. He didn't like hearing that Jake could trust his brother with his life but obviously not his mate.

"I understand, and I look forward to catching up with Alex at the next Alpha meeting. Now to business. I assume you have questions."

Rick laughed, he couldn't help it. "You could say that, Alpha. All my brothers and their mates are extremely anxious to get some answers as well."

Ben frowned, "What do your other brothers have to do with this? Are they just worried about Marcus and Brian?"

Rick shook his head. "Yes, they are worried about Marcus and Brian but my brothers, Alex and Simon, and their mates, Jason and Zack, are a little apprehensive as you can imagine."

Ben looked thoughtful when Rick stopped talking. "Let me get this straight, all your brothers are gay. Is that correct?" he asked.

"Yes."

"Are you gay, Patrick?"

"Please call me Rick, everyone does," he answered. Rick glanced over at Jake but the other man was looking directly at the Alpha, his face a mask, not showing the slightest hint of emotion. Ben was still watching him, waiting. "To answer your question—yes, I am also gay."

"Well, that's interesting. Are you by chance also mated?"

Rick flinched at the question, he didn't mean to but couldn't help it. "No, Ben, I don't have a mate." He refused to look at Jake again.

"I've never heard of an entire family of brothers being gay before. That's very interesting." Rick was confused. What did his brothers all being gay have to do with anything?

He must have looked as confused as he felt. "The gay population of Australia is thought to be roughly three per cent. In comparison, for werewolves it is much lower. Maybe one in every one hundred fifty born. So to have four gay sons so close together is really quite remarkable. And the fact that three of your brothers have found their mates makes it even more so."

Okay, Rick could understand that. He didn't realise how rare it was to be a gay werewolf.

Ben continued. "It didn't used to be this way. Back thousands of years ago when the gods created the first weres there wasn't any stigma attached to having a same sex coupling. It is written that the gods noticed this fact and to ensure the continuation of the species they granted the ability to carry a child to both men and women.

"As the years went by society changed its views on homosexuality and fewer and fewer gay werewolves were born. Due to this fact, the knowledge was lost along the way and very few people today are aware that male weres can get pregnant."

"Holy cow," Rick exclaimed as the breath he didn't know he was holding exploded from his body.

"Okay, so that explains where it started and why we didn't know. Can you tell us how it happens?" Jake asked, speaking up for the first time since this conversation started.

"Well, I imagine it happens the same way it does in straight couples, by inserting a certain appendage into a certain hole," Ben replied with an impish grin.

Rick laughed again. He liked the Alpha, he wasn't at all the stuck up pompous man he was expecting.

"Not exactly what I meant," Jake answered, a slight tinge of pink dusting his cheeks.

"I know but couldn't help myself," Ben replied. "From the information I have gathered, there is a pheromone our body produces once we mate signifying its readiness to have young. If both partners are producing this, and consummate their relationship during a new moon then the possibility of becoming pregnant is highly likely."

"Can they only get pregnant during a new moon?" Jake asked

"Yes, only on the one day a month when the lunar pull is at its lowest." Ben turned his gaze back towards Rick. "I suggest you tell your brothers if they don't want to become fathers to abstain from sex for that one day every month."

Jake laughed this time. "That'll likely kill the lot of them."

Rick chuckled at that. "He's right, you know. A hornier bunch of men I've never met." Ben joined in with their laughter.

Once the laughter died down, Jake got back on track. "Do you know how the whole male pregnancy thing works? As far as I thought, men didn't have the right equipment to carry a child."

"You're right, human men don't. We, however, have the ability to create a temporary womb in our bodies. As we're shifters, our body is used to changing its shape and has no trouble realigning its organs and bones to do this. So when the womb is created our internal organs shift slightly to make room for the baby."

Rick's head was spinning. This was a hell of a lot of information to be dealing with. "Now as I told your brother, the pregnancy usually lasts approximately eighteen weeks, each trimester being only six instead of the thirteen weeks with humans."

"Once the pregnancy is full term, the father will go into labour just like anyone else would. The baby is usually born by caesarean though. Once the baby has been delivered the womb detaches itself and is removed."

"This isn't a one shot deal. You don't only get one chance to be parents. The womb does regrow. However, our bodies develop a natural contraceptive after the trauma of birth and won't allow us to become pregnant again for two years. This gives us not only time to heal but also time to bond with our cubs."

"That makes sense seeing as how there are two years between each of my brothers," Rick said.

Ben smiled, and then his expression turned grave. "I

don't have to tell you gentlemen how imperative it is that this secret does not get out. I'm afraid that once Brian starts to show he's going to be basically on house arrest until the birth."

"That's understandable. What about shifting though? Can he shift while pregnant?" Rick asked. That was one question none of his brothers had thought to come up with.

"Good question. The short answer is—I wouldn't recommend it. Adding the stress of shifting your body on top of what it's already going through is not a good idea. The pull of the full moon to shift and run is nearly non-existent until after the birth."

"Once the baby is born give me a call and let me know all the details. I have a member of my pack who can hack into the appropriate databases and lodge all the required information."

Rick and Jake nodded as they stared at one another. That was something else they hadn't thought of. How do you register the birth of your child who has two fathers and no mother?

"I suggest if you don't want your entire pack to know the details of the child's birth you simply state they used a surrogate. I recommend this explanation to any humans as well. I'll leave it up to Alex to decide whether he's comfortable with telling his pack the entire truth. There is one member that will have to be told though—do you have a pack doctor?"

"Yes, Stephanie Owens. She has her own private practice." Jake answered the Alpha's question.

"Good. I will send my doctor back with you on Friday and they can discuss what medical treatment Brian will require."

"Thank you, Ben, we appreciate that," Rick replied.

"Not at all, it's the least I can do. Now do you have any more questions?"

Rick's brain was reeling, he could barely think, let along come up with any more questions. He thought Ben had answered everything his brothers wanted to know, but wasn't a hundred per cent sure.

"I think that's everything. Thank you, Ben," Jake answered for them in his deep smooth voice.

"Wonderful, I'm glad I could fill in the missing pieces for you. I'll have Philip Carter, our doctor, meet you at Liam's house tomorrow morning, ready to fly back with you in the afternoon. If you ever need anything in the future, please call. Now if you'll excuse me, I'm still trying to deal with the aftermath of Alpha Sawyer murdering poor

Lucas and James."

Rick and Jake both stood and shook the Alpha's hand again. "Thank you for your time and hospitality."

"You're welcome. I'll see you gentlemen tonight at the full moon run." Ben said goodbye as he showed them out.

Once Jake and Rick were seated in Liam's borrowed Ute they looked at each other in silence, both still absorbing everything they had learnt. The silence was broken by Jake not long after. "Jesus H Christ, that's a lot of information for one morning." Rick couldn't agree more as Jake started the car and headed them towards Liam's house.

CHAPTER 7

The rest of the day seemed to pass relatively peacefully. Jake had pulled over on their way back to Liam's so they could get a bite to eat. They barely spoke during lunch, but the silence wasn't strained like usual. Jake put it down to everything they had learnt that morning. His head was positively spinning with the information dump. He could just imagine how Patrick was taking all the news.

One thought that had lodged itself into his brain and stubbornly refused to let go was the thought of him and Patrick creating a life together. A little child with Patrick's brown hair and Jake's blue eyes would be hard to resist. Jake didn't care if his child was a boy or a girl. As long as he or she was created out of love between him and his mate he would be one happy and content man.

Jake knew the dream would never come true and he tried his hardest to dislodge the thought but it wouldn't budge. If he couldn't remove the thought he decided to try and drown it out by watching a mindless movie. This didn't help as Patrick soon joined him and he ended up watching Patrick more than the movie. He was glad Patrick didn't ask him what he thought when it finished as he honestly couldn't have said what the movie was even about.

Liam arrived home in the afternoon and they all sat and had a quiet dinner together. Once they'd finished they locked up and Liam drove them to the state forest where the pack ran on full moons. Jake noticed the sheer number of cars in the parking lot. There were nearly three to four times as many as usually attended the runs at home. Once Liam parked they exited the car and Jake and Patrick followed Liam down a windy path before they turned off and headed through the forest for nearly ten minutes.

The clearing they arrived at was huge and packed with people all mingling around. Liam left them to the side as he went to join his Alpha. Five minutes later the meeting started. Ben made note to welcome Jake and Patrick along with the three other Alphas that were also in attendance. He then settled into pack business. Welcoming new members, acknowledging new matings, and babies born. He heard any complaints and answered any questions his pack had. The entire meeting lasted nearly two hours.

By the time the meeting was finally wrapping up the moon was high in the sky and Jake was itching to shift and run. When Ben gave his blessing for the pack to run Jake didn't stop to think, he simply stripped his shirt off over his head and reached for the buttons on his jeans.

It wasn't until a fingertip lightly touched his back

and the quick indrawn breath behind him that he registered what he had done. Jake quickly spun around so he was facing Patrick, but by the look on the other man's face he knew it was too late and he had seen. *Shit, shit, fucking shit!* Jake silently cursed. Patrick was standing in front of him his hand still extended where he had traced his back, his eyes wide and his mouth parted in surprise.

"What?" It seemed the only word he was able to get out in his surprise. "It's not what you think." Jake cringed. He knew that was the wrong thing to say.

Patrick seemed to shake his head, trying to gather his thoughts. "It's not what I think, huh? What I think is that you have my name tattooed down your spine. My fucking name! And you're standing there trying to tell me it's not what I think? How many other Patricks do you know?" Jake could tell Patrick was getting angry, he didn't blame the man one bit either.

"You're the only Patrick I know," he answered quietly.

Patrick nodded as if he expected that answer. "Why?" was the only word he said.

Jake sighed, he knew he owed Patrick an explanation but it wasn't as easy as he wished. Deciding to tell him some of the truth Jake looked his mate in the eyes.

"You're my mate, and if I couldn't have you then I wanted your name on my body so you would always be close to me."

Patrick swallowed as his eyes filled with tears. Jake watched as the man in front of him quickly stripped his clothes before shifting and taking off into the woods. Jake let a tear silently fall down his cheek. His urge to run now nearly non-existent.

Jake was startled when a hand clapped down on his shoulder. "Nice tat," Liam said as he stepped up beside him. The last thing Jake wanted at the moment was to fight with Liam too.

"I don't know why you haven't claimed your mate yet but the waiting is killing both of you. Grow some balls, man, and claim that which is yours. You'll both be a lot happier when you do."

Jake snapped. "You think it's that easy? It's not!" He practically yelled. "I've had to sit back for the last ten years and watch my mate, knowing I couldn't be with him. I've longed for that man like you couldn't believe. But if I claim him then I put his life in danger and I can't do that."

"I think you need to give Patrick the choice. That man wants nothing else in this world but you. Claim your mate, Jake, you can work everything else out afterwards.

Trust me." And with that Liam too shifted and took off towards the trees.

Jake exhaled, all the fight seemed to leave his body with his breath. He had fought the pull for ten long years, enough was enough. Jake finished shucking his clothes and shifted. He lifted his head and howled out to the moon and his mate, letting them both know he was coming.

* * * *

Rick ran. He didn't care in which direction he headed, he just needed to get as far away from Jake as possible at the moment. The trees and bushes all seemed to blur together as one as he streaked through the forest. The silent night was suddenly broken by a single heartbroken howl. Rick stopped and lifted his face to the sky, sniffing at the air, trying to differentiate the various scents bombarding him.

The howl came again, this time closer. Rick lifted his muzzle to the moon and let his own howl answer, then he took off again. Rick raced through the forest, knowing Jake would catch up to him. He wanted to make it as difficult as possible. He ran for another five minutes before he started to hear the sounds of someone following him.

Jake seemed cautious in his approach. He stayed back, running just behind his left rear flank, following his lead for at least a half hour. Breaking through a dense scrub of trees Rick stumbled across a small clearing with a stream trickling through at the edge.

Rick slowed and walked to the stream, panting he stopped and lapped at the water for several minutes. Jake came to a stop beside him and sat on his haunches as he lowered his head so he too could take a drink.

Once his thirst was quenched, Rick sat back and looked at Jake. He tilted his head to the side, wondering exactly why the other wolf was there. Jake stepped forward and ducked his head, his tongue darting out to lick Rick's muzzle. Rick was shocked. That had to be the last thing he'd expected Jake to do. Rick bared his teeth at Jake and growled. He'd had enough of Jake's games and just wished everything would go away.

Jake ignored his growl and licked him again. Enough was enough, he braced his back legs then lunged at the other wolf. Jake had obviously been expecting this as he easily sidestepped him. Not deterred, Rick spun around to once again face his opponent. He never thought he would be fighting with Jake like this.

He lunged again, this time Jake wasn't quite fast

enough and Rick clamped his jaws down on his hind leg. Jake let out a small yelp of pain before getting free. He tackled Rick to the ground and gently clamped his jaws down on his throat. Rick lay there on his back staring up as Jake positioned himself over his body. Jake growled low in his throat, the sound sending shivers through Rick's entire body. He wanted nothing else in this world but to submit to this wolf. With that in mind, Rick shifted back to human.

By the time he was human again there was a very naked Jake lying on top of his very naked body. Rick gasped as the feeling of their hard cocks rubbing against each other sent shockwaves down his spine, directly to his balls. "Jake—" Rick managed to whisper before his mouth was captured and a searching tongue invaded. Rick lost himself in the sight, the scent and the feel of his mate finally in his arms, and gave into Jake's demanding kiss.

Rick wrenched his head back as he thrust his hips up, he cried out as his orgasm exploded from his body. He had never felt anything so powerful before. Rick never once took his eyes from the man above him, scared that if he closed his eyes this would all be a dream and Jake would disappear.

"So sexy," Jake growled as he leant down and covered Rick's mouth again. Rick's cock had finally stopped twitching and he could feel the copious amounts of seed covering his and Jake's lower abdomens. Jake broke the kiss this time and made his way down his throat, licking over his pulse point before gently placing a kiss against the pounding piece of flesh.

Jake's hands ran up his body causing goose bumps to break out across his skin. Reaching his hard aching nipples, Jake took one erect nub in his mouth, tugging and lapping at the taut piece of flesh. Jake's fingers found his other nipple and began to torture it in conjunction with the first.

Rick cried out at the pleasure racing though his body. Lifting his hands he fisted them in Jake's hair, not sure if he wanted to pull his head away or closer. His cock had filled to hard and aching again and wanted attention. Rick bucked his hips, Jake pulled away from his nipple with a chuckle. "Impatient much?"

"Stop teasing and fuck me," Rick bit out.

"I've waiting a long time to get my hands on your delectable body. I'm not about to rush through this." Before Rick could reply Jake covered his lips in a scorching kiss. Rick moaned as the flavour that was Jake invaded his mouth. Once Rick's mind had been sufficiently turned to mush, Jake sat back on his heels between his legs. "Turn over." Jake's voice was deep and heavy with lust.

Rick didn't think twice about obeying the command. He scrambled onto his hands and knees and lifted his ass into the air. Jake growled behind him before leaning forward and lightly nipping his right cheek. Rick felt Jake's hands settle on his cheeks before they were gently spread, exposing his most private part to his mate. The low rumbling growl came just before a wet tongue swiped against his hole. Rick jumped, not expecting Jake to touch him there with his tongue.

Jake on the other hand seemed to have no qualms as his tongue took another swipe. Rick moaned as the pleasure seeped into his body. He rocked back as Jake speared his tongue and gently worked its way into his body. Rick shuddered at the feeling of finally having a part of Jake inside him, even if it was his tongue. The three day growth on Jake's face scratched perfectly against his cheeks. Rick reached back and wrapped his fingers tightly around the base of his own cock, trying to stave off his orgasm.

Rocking his body back and forth, Rick was soon fucking himself on Jake's tongue. "That's it, baby. God, you feel good." Rick moaned then cried out as Jake inserted a finger inside, along with his tongue. Stretching him, Jake added a second followed soon after by a third finger. When

Jake removed all appendages from his body Rick whimpered, his hole clenching, desperately wanting to be filled again.

"On your back, sexy. I want to look into your eyes as I take you." Rick whimpered again before turning over. Jake grabbed his legs and pushed them back against his chest, lifting his ass higher. Once Jake was satisfied, he pulled one of his hands away and spat on his fingers. Rubbing his saliva over his long, thick erection Jake once again wrapped his hand around Rick's thigh as he lined himself up.

"I'm sorry, this might burn." Rick nodded as Jake pushed forward slowly. As the head of Jake's cock popped through his muscles Rick gasped. The burn was intense, Jake stilled for a moment to let him get used to the feeling of being so full.

"So tight, you feel amazing around my cock," Jake forced out through gritted teeth.

"Never…" Rick panted as he tried to relax around the shaft that filled him so full. He had never felt anything like this before in his life.

The feral look in Jake's eyes at his admission forced Rick's arousal even higher. Jake slowly started to move again, pushing in a couple of inches before pulling back.

Rick's gasp this time was not from pain but from the pleasure shooting through his body.

Jake continued to work his way in, until finally Rick could feel the scratchy hairs from Jake's groin crushed against his ass. "Jesus Christ, you feel like heaven, Patrick. Sorry, I have to move."

"Please—" Rick begged, he lifted his hands and ran them the entire length of Jake's arms before he locked his hands together behind Jake's neck, pulling the man closer. Jake pulled out until just the head of his cock remained inside Rick's body before he thrust home. Rick cried out his happiness at finally being with his mate, before he pulled Jake's head the couple of inches that currently separated them and claimed his mouth.

Jake set a pounding pace, Rick could tell his wolf was riding him hard as claws started to dig in a little on his thighs and he could feel the fur erupting from his arms. Rick broke the kiss with a gasp and looked up at the man he had loved for so long. The animal lurking just under the surface pulled his beast forth, Rick tilted his neck to the side, silently telling the other man what he wanted.

Jake growled and leant forward. The motion changing the angle of his thrusts and Rick screamed as his prostate was hit over and over. Jake licked his neck before he struck, canines piercing his skin. Rick screamed again as his body was overwhelmed with sensation, before he too struck, sinking his own canines into the pulse point on the side of Jake's neck. His cock erupting with stream after stream of pearly white cum, Rick's ass clamped down on the hard length filling him. Rick released his hold on Jake's neck seconds before the other man tore his head back and howled. Jake's cock hardened further before releasing volley after volley of searing hot cum inside Rick's clenching channel.

Rick collapsed against the ground underneath him, Jake falling forward on top of him. Rick had almost managed to catch his breath when the knot extended from Jake's cock and latched on to his prostate. He moaned as his dick once again spilled its seed between their heaving bodies. Jake moaned above him when Rick's muscles clamped around his dick with his third orgasm of the evening.

Pushing his hands beneath him Jake put some room between them before looking back at Rick. Jake lifted a hand and gently wiped away the tears that Rick had no idea he had spilled. "I'm sorry, I'm so sorry Patrick."

Rick had no idea what Jake was apologising for. He really hoped it wasn't the amazing experience they had just had.

"You're mine, Patrick, I don't care who knows it. I never want to go another day without you in it. Please forgive me," Jake whispered. Rick felt his eyes fill with tears again and he quickly tried to blink them away. His throat tight with emotion, all he could do was nod.

Jake smiled then leant forward and sweetly kissed him, Rick's mind was numb when his mate pulled away. Jake's knot released and he slowly slipped from his body. Rick groaned when Jake pulled out. His ass was tender but he could still feel his man so he was happy.

"I love you, Patrick," Jake whispered in his ear as he held him tight against his chest.

"I've waited ten years to hear those words from you." All his emotions seemed to have bubbled up and exploded out along with his orgasm as his eyes filled yet again with tears. He didn't try to hold them back this time though.

Jake gently wiped them away while he continued to hold him close. "I love you too, Jay," Rick whimpered when he was able. Jake seemed to shudder in his arms at his words before he let out a huge sigh and slowly pulled back.

"Come on, we should probably head back. We've

been gone a while." Jake stood, then held his hand out to help Rick to his feet. When Rick was standing Jake tugged until he had Rick tucked in against his chest. He wrapped his arms around Jake's waist and settled his head in the hollow at the base of his neck, breathing in the unmistakable scent of his man and sex. Sighing, he was happy for the first time in ten years and Rick never wanted to let go.

"*Come on, babe*," Jake whispered in his mind as he kissed his cheek before pulling back. Rick smiled as he reluctantly let go. He never thought something as simple as the mating bond would make him so happy, but just hearing Jake in his head had his heart leaping in joy.

They shifted together and Rick stood still admiring the sleek black wolf in front of him. Jake stepped forward and after rubbing his head against Rick's, worked his way down Rick's neck. Jake gently bit down and Rick whined, so happy his mate was marking him with his scent and bite.

Once Jake was happy with his job he stepped back. *"You smell like me now."* Jake's voice held smug satisfaction.

"Good." With that Jake turned and made his way back towards the forest. He stopped once to make sure Rick was following. Assured his mate ran behind him, Jake took

off. He followed their original scent trail back to the clearing.

Rick noticed as soon as they returned that there were very few people remaining. Next to the piles of clothes belonging to them, a wolf laid waiting. Rick assumed the wolf to be Liam, due to the fact the man was their ride home.

They walked to their clothing and Rick stopped when Jake hunched down and growled at the peaceful looking wolf. The light brown wolf lifted his head and seemed to raise an eyelid in question before shifting back. Liam stood there completely naked and smirking at Jake.

"Calm down, Cujo, I have no designs on your man." Rick huffed out a laugh. Jake, however, didn't find it funny. The man shifted and crossed his arms over his very impressive chest.

"Turn around."

"Excuse me?" Liam looked a little startled at the command.

"There is no way in hell I am letting you see my mate naked, now turn around or I'll turn you around." Jake's voice seemed to drop with the threat and Rick couldn't believe how turned on he was.

"Fine," Liam said, exasperated as he swung around

and reached down to pick up his clothes. Liam started to get dressed with his back to them.

Rick shifted then jumped into Jake's arms, taking his mouth in a deep, hard kiss as he rutted against Jake. Pulling back rather than risking blacking out due to lack of oxygen, Rick looked Jake in the eyes. "God, you're sexy as hell when you're all growly."

He thrust his hips forward again only to have his actions brought to a halt by a hard slap to his ass. "Later, I promise. Now get dressed before I stop caring about who's watching and take this tight ass of yours again." His words were accompanied by a finger sliding down his crease and thrusting fast inside him. Rick cried out in pleasure before Jake pulled his finger away and unwrapped Rick's legs from his waist.

Rick stood there panting hard trying to get his brain into some sort of working order after being denied the pleasure it was desperately seeking. Another slap to his ass had him yipping and jumping forward, his hands quickly rubbing his now smarting rear end.

"Clothes, now." Oh yeah. Rick ignored the laughter coming from Liam as he looked around, spotting his clothes in a pile where he had ripped them off earlier. Once he was sufficiently covered again he made his way back to

Jake and burrowed once again into the man's strong arms.

"Sorry, but I think I'm going to be a very touchy person for a while. I'm still reeling from that fact that you're finally mine." Rick hid his face in Jake's neck as his cheeks heated with his confession. He placed a gentle kiss against Jake's pulse.

"Touch all you want, babe, I'm not going anywhere now."

Liam interrupted their private moment. "Let's head back. It's late and you guys have a flight to catch tomorrow." Rick pulled back but never completely let go of Jake as they made their way through the trees to the car park. Jake settled into the back seat of Liam's sedan with him, Jake's arm wrapped around his shoulder pulling him tight against his side.

Rick fisted his hands in Jake's shirt and attached his mouth to his neck, not caring about the man in the front seat. He sucked and nibbled on Jake's neck until he was satisfied with the dark purple bruise that glistened with his saliva. The noises Jake made as Rick attacked his neck had him hard and aching in no time and wishing for nothing else in this world but the ability to have another orgasm brought forth by the man in his arms.

CHAPTER 8

Jake's cock strained against his fly, hard enough to pound nails. Patrick's mouth on his throat drove him out of his mind. Jake tilted his head to give Patrick more room to move as he cupped the back of his head gently and pushed the man closer against his neck. He loved the fact that Patrick had marked him.

A throat clearing brought his thoughts back to the other man in the car. Blinking to clear his vision, he focused his gaze on Liam.

"We're home. You might want to move things inside." The laugher was clearly evident in his voice.

Jake didn't bother to respond, but thought the man's idea was brilliant. His mate in a comfortable bed and a bottle of lube sounded like his idea of paradise. Jake laughed when he tried to pull away from Patrick and the man just followed him, whimpering. He rummaged around beside him until he felt the door handle. Opening the door he made his way out of the back seat, careful not to detach Patrick from his side.

Once Jake had his feet under him he picked Patrick up in his arms. Wrapping the man's legs around his waist, he settled his hands under Patrick's delectable ass, squeezing the cheeks tightly as he made his way into the house and down the hall.

Jake didn't see Liam again and once he was inside his room he closed the door behind him and crawled, with Patrick still wrapped tight around his body, onto the bed. Patrick finally loosened his hold when his back lay flat against the mattress. Jake took the opportunity to sit up and start stripping the clothes from his body. Patrick caught on quickly and they were soon a mass of arms and legs as they attempted to get naked in a hurry.

Jake sat and admired the beautiful body of his mate. Light tanned skin, fine hair leading down to six pack abs and a stunning, thin, long cock straining for attention. Jake licked his lips before he dove forward and swallowed his mate down. It had been a while since he had sucked a cock but he remembered how, and put all his skills to use now.

He knew Rick would still be tender after his first time in the forest, especially considering he'd used nothing but saliva to ease his entry. Jake sucked around the length in his mouth before easing back up to the head. Patrick moaned his pleasure and threaded his hands into Jake's hair, trying to hold him down.

Jake flicked his tongue out and swiped it through the slit at the tip of his mate's cock. He groaned as the intense flavour of his mate burst across his tastebuds. Hollowing his cheeks Jake slid down the length of his mate's shaft, loving the feeling of Patrick being in his mouth.

His hands, wanting to explore his mate's body, made their way across naked skin. One tugged and pulled and pinched Patrick's light brown coloured nipples, while the other explored his mate's thighs before gently cupping his tightly drawn sac.

Jake pulled off the hard shaft for a moment as he sucked a finger into his mouth. Making sure the digit was nice and wet, he removed it from his mouth and turned his attention back to the flushed, leaking cock in front of him. Drawing the length back between his lips, Jake slipped his wet finger behind his mate's sac and followed the trail down until he came to the quivering entrance awaiting his touch.

Jake increased his suction and speed as he speared his finger to the first knuckle into Patrick's tight entrance. Patrick screamed above him and the hands in his hair tightened their grip as he thrust forward and unloaded into Jake's mouth. Jake sucked down spurt after spurt of his mate's delicious seed until the man lay quivering and sated beneath him.

Giving the cock in his mouth one final lick, Jake pulled off and sat up. He quickly made his way up Patrick's body until he was straddling his hips. Jake took hold of his hard, aching shaft and started tugging on it at a furious pace. A half a dozen strokes were all it took before Jake was crying out his release and watching as he painted his cum all over Patrick's body.

Collapsing forward on to one hand, his other still wrapped tight around his softening cock, Jake ducked his head and took possession of Patrick's lips.

Patrick pulled away from the kiss after several minutes and smiled at him. "Umm… I'm a little sticky."

Jake couldn't help but laugh. "I believe you're correct. Stay there, I'll go get a cloth to clean you up." With that, Jake placed a quick hard kiss on Patrick's lips before he jumped from the bed and headed to the door. He looked to make sure Liam wasn't still up before he made his way to the bathroom. Jake wet a cloth with warm water and quickly cleaned himself before rinsing the face washer and making his way back to the bedroom.

Slipping back into his room, Jake was momentarily stunned at the beauty of Patrick lying naked in his bed. Snapping out of his thoughts he climbed back onto the bed and gently cleaned their combined fluids from Patrick's body.

Once he was happy his mate would no longer be 'sticky' Jake threw the face washer on the floor and snuggled up behind the man he loved, pulling the blankets up around him as he did.

Jake kissed the back of Patrick's neck as he pulled the man closer against his chest and settled down to sleep. Ten minutes later he had started to drift off when he was woken by a very tentative voice in his head, whispering one word.

"*Why?*"

Jake decided after all this time Patrick had a right to know what had happened and why it had taken him so long to claim his mate. Pulling back, Jake sat up and settled against the headboard of the bed.

Patrick was watching him curiously, until Jake held out his arms. Patrick moved across the distance between them quickly and snuggled back into Jake's arms. If he was going to tell this tale he would do it with the man he loved in his arms.

* * * *

Ten Years Ago

Jake stretched as he got out of his beat up old Toyota. It was good to be back in his hometown again and he was looking forward to catching up with his best friend. He had gotten home last night after another six month stint at the University of Melbourne. He was studying for his masters in commercial law and had another eighteen months' worth of study ahead of him.

But at the moment it was mid-semester break and Jake had come home. He wanted to see his parents, his friends and run with his pack. That, especially, Jake had missed. Living in the heart of a large city for most of the previous few years while he was studying caused issues with his inner wolf. There isn't a great deal of land in cities a were was able to shift and run during the full moon.

He was really looking forward to running with his pack once again. Speaking of pack, Jake looked up at the house of his Alpha, Joe Holland. Alex, his best friend, was the Alpha's oldest child, they had four sons in total. Alex had no idea he was home for the holidays yet. He had gotten in late last night and thought to surprise his friend this morning.

Jake walked up the brick pathway, noticing there were no cars parked in the drive. He wondered if anyone was actually home. If not, he would just call his friend and find out where the hell he was. Excited now to see his Alex, Jake quickened his pace, until he found himself standing before the door.

Lifting his knuckles he rapped loudly on the solid wood door three times before taking a step back and waiting. Jake frowned when the door wasn't immediately opened and realised his surprise wasn't going to work as no one was home. Turning around to head back to his car, Jake had only taken two steps when he heard the unmistakable sound of the door swinging open.

Jake swung around expecting to see his best friend standing in the doorway. Instead he was confronted with the sight of a much younger Holland brother; an extremely sexy and delicious smelling, much younger Holland brother.

Jake shook his head to try and clear the lust that was currently coursing through his entire body. The only thing this seemed to do was to stir the air around him and allow the most wonderful scent he had ever smelt in his life to permeate every pore in his body. Jake groaned as his cock hardened to just this side of painful in his jeans, and his gums itched as his canines threatened to extend.

He had never lost control of his wolf before, but

staring at the young man in front of him was causing all sorts of internal struggles to take place. Jake had always been especially drawn to Patrick, but with the cub being so much younger than him, he had kept his distance. Now his wolf wanted that distance to disappear altogether.

Before he knew what was happening Jake found himself with his arms full of hot, horny teenager, as Patrick attempted to climb his body. Jake moaned as their hard shafts rubbed against each other as Patrick's lips found his. His arms around the young man currently wrapped around his body, Jake took control of the kiss.

He staggered back towards the house until he had Patrick pushed up against the wall. His wolf was howling its approval of the situation. Jake's brain finally kicked back into gear and he remembered exactly who it was he was practically molesting against the front of his Alpha's house.

Breaking the kiss, Jake looked down into the shocked eyes of the man in his arms. Nearly black eyes stared back at him, heavy with lust and what he thought looked suspiciously like love. Shaking his head Jake tried to take a step back, only to realise Patrick was still wrapped around him.

"Mate," Patrick whispered at him.

"Shit!" Jake couldn't help the expletive from passing his lips. He didn't expect this when he came home from uni. Jake's heart skipped a beat as the happy, excited expression slipped from Patrick's face and his legs slipped from around his waist.

Wanting nothing more than to see his mate smile, and Jake couldn't deny the fact that the younger cub was his mate when his entire being was screaming the truth of the word, he cupped Patrick's face in his hands and gently pecked his lips in another kiss.

"Is anyone else home?" he asked wanting to move this from the front where everyone could see.

Patrick just shook his head. Jake grabbed his hand and led the youth into the house. He needed to go somewhere he wouldn't be tempted to ravish the barely legal young man. He knew the age of consent in the state was sixteen, but he was still six years older than Patrick and the thought was just wrong as far as he was concerned.

Looking around, he decided the lounge room with its large couch was definitely out, as were any of the bedrooms. That left the dining room and the kitchen, they seemed safe enough.

Jake took a seat at the head of the table, while Patrick sat in the chair to his right. He never once let go of

Jake's hand, which he was more than happy about. His mate may be young but he was still his and Jake wanted to touch as much as he was allowed.

"So, this is a surprise." Talk about stating the obvious, but Jake was still in shock.

Patrick laughed and the sound shot straight to Jake's cock. Patrick's entire face lit up with the laughter and Jake wanted to see his mate laugh every day, just so he could see that expression.

"I didn't realise the mating instinct would kick in when I turned sixteen." Patrick blushed and ducked his head, shy all of a sudden. Jake groaned as his cock throbbed. "I've always had a crush on you," Patrick admitted so quietly, that, if it wasn't for his superior hearing Jake would have missed it.

Jake tucked a knuckle under Patrick's chin and lifted his face, so he could once again look his mate in the eyes. He knew he wasn't going to like what Jake was about to say. "I can't claim you yet."

Patrick's eyes widened and his mouth opened in shock. "Please hear me out, baby." Jake cursed the endearment as soon as it slipped passed his tongue. "You're only sixteen. I'm six years older than you, and I'll be leaving again in a week to go back to Melbourne for uni. If

I claim you now, I wouldn't be able to leave you behind and I can't take you with me; you still have school here to complete."

Patrick looked so sad but he nodded his understanding. "I'm not saying I won't claim you, we just need to give it time." Jake pulled Patrick forward and kissed his mate, trying to reassure the youth.

Breaking the kiss, another thought entered his head. "Fuck, your brother and your dad are going to kill me." He groaned at the thought of telling Alex his youngest brother was his mate.

Patrick laughed again, the light tinkling sound seeped into his skin. "I won't tell them until you're willing to claim me, how's that?"

"You don't have to do that, Patrick. I don't mind if you want to tell them, they're your family," Jake said carefully.

"I know I don't have to, Jay, but I want to." The sound of the nickname Patrick had given him years ago, said in his soft voice, sent shivers down his spine. "I want to keep you all to myself for the time being. If no one else knows then you're all mine." Patrick's cheeks turned pink. Jake was starting to love the look.

Patrick rubbed his hand over the stubble on his

cheek. Jake had been lazy since he finished school and hadn't shaved in several days. "I like this look on you, it makes you look even sexier than before."

"I should head off before your family gets home and finds me ravishing you." The lust in his voice was making it even deeper than usual.

"You can ravish me anytime you want," Patrick offered.

Jake wasn't strong enough not to bring their lips together and once more take control of the other man's mouth. He thrust his tongue past Patrick's lips and growled at the taste. He slowly gentled the kiss until he pulled back completely.

"Have you got your own phone?" Jake asked when he once more had the power of speech. Patrick nodded and gave him his number. "I'll call you tomorrow," he said as he stood.

"I'd like that." Patrick stood and they walked through the house to the front door in silence.

Cupping Patrick's cheek, Jack placed a gentle kiss across the kiss-swollen lips. "Be good," he whispered before he turned and left the house. He didn't look back as he didn't think he would be able to leave if he saw his mate watching him walk away.

Jake got in his car and drove to the pack running grounds. He had excess energy to burn and his wolf was demanding to be let out. His was the only car in the car park as he pulled up and got out. Jake stripped where he was, as there was no one else around, and walked into the bush. He shifted then ran. Several hours later his thoughts were still stuck on the fact that he had met his mate, his very young and inexperienced mate.

The idea of being Patrick's only lover brought forth a howl of possessiveness. He loved the fact that no other man would ever get the opportunity to touch his man. It was going to kill him to not be near Patrick, now that he knew what the young man was to him. He had to talk to his father and let the man know he had found his mate, even if he couldn't claim him yet.

Exhausted after his run, Jake took his time making his way back to his dad's house.

His mum had walked out several years ago and had left him behind. His parents hadn't been a mated pair. Jake unlocked the door and made his way through the house to his room. He didn't see the point of having his own place when he was only here for a couple of weeks. He stripped his clothes once again and headed for the bathroom.

Jake stopped to look in the mirror. He knew it was

silly but if Patrick liked him with stubble then he would keep it. He would have to buy a shaver to keep it to the length he wanted as he didn't want to be sporting a full beard. That look wouldn't suit him at all, he didn't think.

Turning the water on to heat up Jake palmed his still hard cock and watched as a bead of pre-cum appeared at the tip. Jake stepped into the shower and hissed as the hard spray hit his aching shaft. Patrick's scent had made him hard that morning and he had been that way ever since, now he could finally do something about it.

He grabbed the conditioner from the shelf and squirted a generous amount in his hand before wrapping his fist around his cock and squeezing hard. Jake moaned as lightning bolts of arousal shot through his body. His thoughts were firmly back on Patrick wrapped around his body as their mouths met in a spine melting kiss.

Jake's hand increased its speed, knowing he wouldn't last long, he had been on edge for hours. Remembering the feeling of Patrick's hard shaft rubbing against his own sent Jake careening over the edge, his mate's name called out at the exact moment of ecstasy when his cock erupted. Jake placed his palm against the wall as he attempted to keep his legs from buckling as the last shudders of his orgasm left his body.

Once Jake was sure he could stand without his legs giving way he quickly washed his body and stepped out of the shower. He dried himself then made his way back to his room. Jake collapsed face-down on his bed and succumbed to the exhaustion sweeping though his body.

Jake startled awake several hours later as the front door was slammed shut. His dad was home and it didn't seem as if he was in a good mood. He wondered how his father would take the news that he had found his mate. Alex had come out several years ago and his dad had told him to each his own, so Jake thought his dad should be fine with his own sexuality.

He had never really thought about coming out himself as Jake enjoyed a very well-rounded sex life. If he was honest with himself then he would be forced to admit that he enjoyed his encounters with other men more than with the women he slept with.

Jake dressed in silence and made his way down the hall, looking for his dad, Arthur Richmond.

He found him in the living room sitting in his favourite chair watching the news. "Hey Dad, bad day at the office?"

"Yeah, you could say that, son. Pizza for dinner

okay?" His dad was a large man, thick black hair and wide shoulders. He had sharp cheekbones and his five o'clock shadow was as dark as the hair on his head. He was also the third most powerful wolf in their pack, after the Alpha and Beta.

"That's fine, you want me to order?" Jake took the nod as assent and went to get the phone. He placed their order for pizza and went to join his father. Wanting to give his father time to relax, Jake decided to wait 'til after they had eaten to bring up his new discovery.

Jake watched the television with his dad until the doorbell rang. He paid for their dinner, grabbed a couple of plates and went back to the living room. They ate in silence until the entire pizza was gone.

Gathering his courage Jake turned to face his father. "Dad, can we talk?"

His father muted the television before turning in his seat to face him. They were catty-corner to each other with Jake sitting on the couch. "Sure son. How's school going?"

"Fine, Dad, school's going well. It's a lot of information to take in, but I'm doing well." Jack looked his father in the eye. "That's not what I want to talk to you about though."

His dad looked a little shocked but his expression

still showed love and acceptance of whatever Jake wanted to talk about. "Okay then, what's on your mind?"

Jake sucked in a deep breath then let it out. It was like ripping off a Band-Aid. "I found my mate." Okay, so maybe not.

His dad's expression showed nothing but joy. "That's great! Where is she? Why didn't you bring her home with you?" He was looking around like he expected someone else to just walk out from around a corner.

Jake winced at his dad's assumption about the sex of his mate. "It's a little more complicated than that, Dad."

"What's complicated? You claim her and bring her home to meet me."

"Dad, my mate is Patrick Holland, and he's only sixteen. That's why it's complicated." Jake watched as the love and joy on his father's face changed instantly to anger and hatred. Jake was startled at his father's expression.

"Your mate is who?" His dad screamed at him.

"Patrick Holland, the Alpha's youngest son." Jake hoped that the mention of their Alpha might calm his father down but he was mistaken.

Arthur Richmond seemed to get even angrier. "I forbid you to claim him."

Shock coursed through Jake's body as he sat back

quickly. God, he hoped he had misunderstood what his father had said. "Dad, Patrick's only sixteen. I've already told him I won't claim him until I finish school at least."

All Jake's hopes died at his father's next words. "I don't care how old the kid is," his father answered, practically biting off each word through clenched teeth. "You. Are. Not. Going. To. Claim. Him. I. Forbid. It."

Jake looked at his father, face red with rage, hands in white knuckled fists, his chest heaving with every breath he took. He had never seen his dad like this. "Why?" he asked since he couldn't get his head around why his father was so against his mate.

"You are not gay. You will never be gay. I don't care what your friends do with their lives, but my son will not lower himself to be a god damn sodomite." Jake shook his head trying to understand where all this sudden anger and hatred had come from. Had his dad always been like this and he had just never seen it?

"Dad, Patrick is my mate. It doesn't matter what gender he is, I have to claim him." Jake tried again, pleading with his father to understand.

Before he could even blink his father was out of his chair and had Jake off the couch and pressed against the wall with his fist wrapped around his throat. Claws dug into his skin as his dad pressed tight, Jake could feel the trickle of blood run down his neck.

His father stood with his face mere centimetres from his own, not once letting up the grip around his throat. Jake could barely breathe and what little air he did have drained from his body at his dad's next words. "Now you listen to me and you listen good." Arthur Richmond shook him before continuing. "You lay one hand on your so-called mate and I will kill the little fucker. I don't care who his father is."

All the blood drained from face at the same time as the air expelled from his lungs. Jake couldn't believe what he had just heard. "You run and tell anyone else that he's your mate and I kill him. I will not have a fag for my son, do you understand me?" Jake could barely move, he was pinned so tight against the wall. "I have no problem with carrying out my threat against the little shit so you better take me seriously."

A minute nod of the head was all Jake could manage. His father spat in his face as he stepped back. "Get out of my sight."

Jake doubled over, heaving to gain precious oxygen back into his lungs. Once sure he could move, Jake stood straight and looked his father in the eyes for probably the last time. "If you touch a hair on Patrick's head, I will kill you myself."

Jake turned to make his way to his bedroom. He heard his father call out behind him, "That may be so, son, but it won't stop your so-called mate from being dead." Jake ignored his father and collapsed back on the bed as his mind processed everything he had lost that night.

Hours later he heard his father moving around getting ready for bed. When everything was once again quiet and he was sure his dad was asleep. Jake packed everything he wanted to keep and left. He wouldn't ever be going back to that house again as long as his father was alive.

He loaded his car up and drove away. Jake wiped at the tears that ran down his cheeks as he made it to the town limits. He had to call Patrick. He knew it was late but hopefully his mate would have his phone close by. Jake pulled over and stared at the name of his mate in his phone. The screen blurred behind his tears, Jake angrily wiped them away. He couldn't do this if he was crying. Gathering all the courage he had he pressed the button to connect the call.

Jake knew if he saw Patrick again he would ask the young cub to go with him, and that wasn't fair to either of them or Patrick's parents. This was the only thing Jake could think to do to keep his mate safe from his father.

The call connected after a couple of rings and his mate's sleepy voice sounded, "Hello?" The word was almost slurred. Jake had to stop himself from smiling.

"Patrick—" Jake's throat closed in refusal to let out anything else.

"Jay?" Jake could hear rustling in the background as his mate moved in bed.

"Listen, Patrick," Jake tried again. Forcing his throat to cooperate. "I've thought about things and we can't be together."

"I know that, Jay, you said that this afternoon. When I finish school and you come back from uni for good we can be together then." The hope and longing in Patrick's voice was evident.

Jake shook his head even though the other man couldn't see him. "No, Patrick," Jake forced himself to continue, "we can't be together, ever. I don't want you as my mate." It was the hardest thing Jake had ever said.

The quick indrawn breath on the other end of the line nearly broke his heart. "What?" The word broke on the end of a sob and Jake hated himself for putting his young innocent mate through this.

"I don't want you as my mate. I'm heading back to uni tonight. Please don't call me."

"No, wait, please Jay, can't we talk about this? We're fated to be together. I love you." His mate's quiet sobs shattered what remained of his heart. Jake managed to squeeze out one more word, "No," before he hung up the phone and broke down. Jake turned his phone off when it started to ring as he couldn't handle seeing his mate's name on the screen.

Jake wiped his eyes a short time later and put the car in gear. He had a life to get back to. It may be one filled with loneliness from now on, and a broken heart, but Jake would be back.

He couldn't stay away from his mate no matter what his father said. When he finished school he would be back to watch over Patrick and make sure his father never laid a hand on a single hair on Patrick's head. With that plan now in place Jake took off on the dark road back to Melbourne.

A week later, he was back on campus sporting a brand new tattoo and waiting for the first lecture of the semester to begin.

* * * *

Rick didn't know what to say. He never thought the reason Jake and he weren't together was because his mate's father had threatened his life. So he didn't say anything, instead he tightened his hold around Jake and held the mate he had been denied for so long.

"I'm so sorry," Jake whispered into his hair.

Rick felt all the emotions from the night he had gotten that horrible phone call resurface and was forced to blink rapidly in order to hold back the tears that threatened. "I cried for two days after that damn call," he said softly. "I scared the hell out of my entire family because I wouldn't tell them what was wrong. Even after everything, I couldn't do that to you. If you didn't want me that was your choice, but I didn't want you to lose Alex as well."

Jake's arms tightened around him. "I don't deserve you," he said. "And there hasn't been a day that's gone by in the last ten years that I haven't wanted you."

"What are we going to do about your dad?" That was the question that worried Rick the most, he didn't want Jake to get hurt.

"I don't know yet. We'll deal with that when we get home. For now it's late, how about we get some sleep?"

Jake scooted down until he was once again lying on the bed, never once did he remove his hold from around

Rick. Rick sighed, happy and content for the first time in ten years. He placed a kiss on Jake's neck then closed his eyes and let sleep take him away, everything else could wait.

CHAPTER 9

Rick felt like he had only just closed his eyes when someone was shaking him trying to get him to wake up.

"Go away," he slurred as his brain attempted to shut back down, ready for more sleep.

"Nope, time to get up. I want to show you something." Jake sounded way too cheerful for this time of morning.

Rick cracked an eye open and looked at the curtains. Still dark outside, not even a speck of light broke through the fabric. "Go away, 'm sleeping," he said again as he pulled the covers tighter around him.

Jake laughed, then Rick was suddenly cold as the covers were ripped from his grip and a hard hand landed on his ass. Rick yelped at the slap and moved his hands to cover his rear end. "What the hell?"

Jake just laughed again. The man was far too chipper for this time of day. "Get out of bed and get dressed, we're going for a jog."

"No way in hell, man, it's not even light out! Now give me back the covers." Rick was usually a morning person, but this was ridiculous. The sun had to be at least up before he would even consider getting out of bed.

Jake threw his clothes at him and when Rick moved his hands to catch the offending garments Jake slapped his ass again. "Come on, Patrick, if we don't leave soon we'll miss it and I really want you to see this before we leave."

Rick grumbled as he sat up in bed. Jake was lucky he was so sexy, otherwise there would be hell to pay. The man in question walked over to him and kissed him good morning.

"Stop pouting and I'll blow you in the shower when we get back," Jake said as he stood up and winked at him. Rick's cock took immediate interest in the promise and wondered if they could skip everything else and go directly to the shower.

His thoughts must have been clearly spelt out on his face and Jake chuckled. "Nope, jog, shower, then blowjob, in that order. I'll meet you at the front door in two minutes, don't be late." With that, Jake turned and strode from the room.

Sighing in resignation, Rick quickly dressed and found his shoes. Once he was ready he joined Jake at the front door. Jake gave him another kiss before the pair made their way outside. "Where exactly are we going?" Rick asked as they stretched their muscles. He wasn't like his brothers, he didn't enjoy running all that much in human form. He preferred to keep his running to the four legged variety.

Jake pasted on a wicked smile, which Rick was sure would turn his insides to mush. "You'll see." And with that Jake took off. Shaking his head he took off after his mate, down the dark street.

A half hour later, Rick was wondering how much farther they had to go. The sun was just starting to light the edges of the sky. Another ten minutes later and they rounded the last bend and Jake came to a stop.

In front of Rick the road continued on into the distance, surrounded on each side by endless fields of sugarcane. The cool crisp morning had left dew clinging to the leaves of the cane stalks, the sun chose that exact moment to break through the darkness. The light shimmered across the entire fields and Rick didn't think he had ever seen anything so spectacular in his life.

Jake stepped behind him and wrapped his arms around his torso, pulling him back against Jake's hard chest. "It's beautiful," Rick whispered, not wanting to break the peacefulness of the sight before him.

"I know. I saw it a couple of day ago and immediately thought of you," Jake whispered back to him. Rick wished he had a camera with him, but knew this was one sight he would remember always.

They stayed standing there staring out over the fields for nearly fifteen minutes, watching as the sun dawned on another day. The first day of their mating and Rick was thankful that Jake had dragged him out of bed so they could start their new lives together this way.

The silence was soon broken by a car speeding down the road. Jake kissed his cheek then pulled back. "Come on, we better head back. We have things to do before we leave."

"Number one on the list is a shower," Rick replied as he wiggled his eyebrows suggestively. Jake laughed then turned and took off back in the direction they had come from. Rick was more than happy to run behind as he got to stare at Jake's glorious ass the entire way home.

* * * *

Alex called after they finished breakfast to confirm that Dr Carter, who would be going back with them to check up on Brian, would be staying with their mum and dad, as they had no room left in their house. The flight home was due to get in at Albury at ten o'clock that night. They then had more than an hour's drive before they got home. It was going to be another late night, but Rick didn't dread the trip home like he had the trip here.

Philip Carter arrived at Liam's house at ten that morning. After the introductions were made they packed the car and Rick made one last survey of the rooms to make sure they hadn't left anything behind. Jake found him standing in the doorway to his room staring at the bed they had slept in together.

The warmth of Jake's body as he stepped up behind Rick settled something deep inside. Rick leant back, resting his head on Jake's shoulder. "Come on, babe, let's go home." Jake's lips pressed against his temple.

They made their way outside hand in hand and Jake held the back door of the car open for him. This was probably the only part of the trip he wasn't looking forward to. Liam locked his house then he and the doc got in the car.

The drive back through the Gillies wasn't nearly as bad as the first time. Rick thought that might have had something to do with the fact that he'd snuggled in close to Jake and closed his eyes and just breathed in the scent of his mate.

Before he knew it they were at the airport and it was time to say goodbye to Liam. Jake grabbed their bags and placed them on the curb beside the car. Liam came up to them and shook their hands in farewell. "Well, guys, it's certainly been interesting having you," he said with amusement evident in his voice. Rick felt his cheeks heat at everything that had happened.

"Thank you for everything. If you ever need anything, you have my number," Rick replied as he pulled the Beta into a quick hug. He ignored the soft growl behind him. Stepping back he watched as Jake offered a gruff thanks before Liam said goodbye to his pack mate and got back in his car.

The trio made their way through the airport to check in, before heading to the departure lounge. During the wait Rick spoke quietly with Dr Carter and found out the man had dealt with a half dozen or so similar cases to Brian's in his thirty years as a pack doctor. Rick was still shocked to hear how rare it was for their kind to be gay.

The flight home was long and Rick was starting to worry about what would happen when they got there. Would Jake go back to his apartment like nothing had happened between them? Was Rick strong enough to cope if Jake once again denied him? Or would he declare their mating to the pack and deal with his father?

"Stop thinking so hard," Jake said to him. "I can

hear your thoughts. You're practically shouting them at me."

"Sorry, didn't mean to." Rick was mortified that Jake had heard all his inner insecurities.

"It's okay. And for the record, I'm coming home with you tonight. We can deal with everything else as it comes up. You're mine now and I won't be parted from you again. Ten years was far too long to go without my mate."

Rick smiled and kissed Jake. The kiss soon turned heated and the sound of a throat clearing brought back exactly where they were. A hostess stood in the middle of the aisle holding a tray of food. Rick blushed and muttered his thanks as he took the tray and placed it down in front of him.

He whacked Jake on the arm when he heard a snicker escape the man's lips. "So not funny." Rick narrowed his eyes at Jake as he seemed to explode with laughter. He huffed and attempted to ignore the other man and concentrate to his food. If his mouth tried to turn up at the corners in his own smile Rick would deny it.

* * * *

It was well past midnight by the time Jake pulled

his car up to the curb out front of Rick's house. Their plane from Sydney to Albury had been delayed, and then they had to drop the doctor off at Joe and Maryanne's place. Joe had informed them that Alex had taken tomorrow off—well, he guessed today as it was now morning—and had organised a family meeting, including their pack doctor to find out the information they had learnt.

Jake just hoped it wasn't set for too early in the morning. He needed some sleep. After everything that had happened in the last several days, his body felt ready to collapse.

Jake shut off the engine and grabbed their bags. The large house in front of him, which he had both dreaded, and loved, visiting over the last ten years, had never looked better. All the windows were black. The entire household was asleep, which was exactly what he planned to do with his mate in his arms.

Jake followed Patrick up to the front door. Once the door was unlocked and they were inside, Jake quietly closed the door and locked it again behind him. He followed his mate down a passageway and into his bedroom. Jake had never been so happy to see a king-size bed in his life. He dropped the suitcase and started stripping.

It was only when he kicked his shoes off that he noticed Patrick had collapsed fully dressed, face first on to the bed. Jake finished getting undressed then walked over to help his tired mate.

Patrick mumbled something into his pillow as Jake stripped him of his clothes. Once they were both naked Jake pulled the sheets out from underneath Patrick then climbed into bed and pulled his mate into his arms. He covered them both with the covers and settled down to sleep. Patrick snuggled in, resting his head on his chest with his arm wrapped tight around his waist. Jake had never been more comfortable in his life as the darkness took him away.

Jake woke to light streaming though the curtain and an empty bed beside him. He climbed out of the nice warm sheets and made his way to the bathroom. Once he had taken care of his bladder, he pulled his jeans on from last night, not bothering to do up the top button.

"Babe?" he asked still not entirely functional yet.

"Kitchen." Jake headed in the direction of his mate and coffee. He walked into the room and right up to his mate who stood pouring a cup of coffee at the kitchen counter. "Hmm. Morning, gorgeous," he said as he leant in and kissed his mate. Patrick seemed to fumble with

something then wrapped his arms around him and melted into the kiss.

"Morning to you too." Patrick chuckled as he broke the kiss. "Take a seat and I'll finish getting you coffee." Jake nodded and turned around only to walk directly into Alex's fist.

Jake's head snapped back as pain radiated from his jaw. "My baby brother? What the fuck, Jake? I sent you away for a reason and that wasn't to seduce my fucking brother." Jake rubbed his jaw as he looked at the pissed off expression on his best friend and Alpha's face.

"It's not what you think." Jake really needed to stop saying those words.

Alex raised an eyebrow. "You have ten seconds to explain to me why you were practically molesting my baby brother in our kitchen before I hit you again." Alex growled at him. His voice was low and dangerous and anyone other than him would probably be scared shitless by now.

Jake looked over his shoulder at Patrick. The man just smiled and blew him a kiss. So not helping. Shit! "This isn't how I planned to tell you but Patrick's my mate." The blood seemed to drain from Alex's face as those words registered in his brain. Alex stared at Patrick, until his eyes narrowed. Jake knew he had spotted the mating mark and sighed, closing his eyes.

That's the only reason he didn't see the second fist coming as it too connected with his already tender jaw. "Shit, man! Would you stop hitting me already?"

Jake took a step back trying to put some distance between them. Jason came up beside Alex and spoke softly into his ear, coaxing the large Alpha back to his seat at the table. Patrick came up beside him and kissed the spot where Alex had connected not once but twice. "You okay, big guy?"

"Yeah, hurts like a son of a bitch, but can't say I blame him for it. I'd probably punch me too if I was in his position."

"Well, I can."

Jake narrowed his eyes at his mate and tried to grab his arm but the man danced out of his reach. Patrick stalked over to the table opposite where his brother sat. He leant over, his fists clenched and pressed against the wood. "If you so much as lay one more hand on my mate, I will cut your balls off while you sleep. Understand me, brother?"

To say everyone was a little shocked at the threat from Patrick was an understatement. Alex growled at his brother before Jason smacked him. "You do it again and I'll help him," Jason said to his mate, arms folded across his chest.

Patrick smirked at his brother and raised an eyebrow.

"Am I the only one here that realises these two didn't just meet?" Alex growled out.

"No, you're not," Brian piped up from where he was sitting at the table. "But their reasons for not mating before are their own, unless they decide to share them."

"Thanks, B." Patrick glanced at his brother-in-law and smiled.

"Is it safe to approach the table?" Jake asked, looking at his friend.

"Fine, but you and I will be talking about this later." Jake nodded, he knew he'd have to explain everything to his friend. He just hoped they could come up with a plan to stop his father before anyone got hurt.

Everyone seemed to settle down as Jake took a seat at the table and breakfast turned into a noisy affair. Jake looked at Brian who had more colour in his face since the last time he had seen the man. Brian seemed to feel his eyes on him and turned to smile at him.

The smile turned cheeky. "Wanna see?"

Jake wasn't sure what the hell he was talking about. His confusion must have been evident as Brian laughed then stood and lifted his shirt and pushed hip pants down until they rested at the top of his pubic area.

It took a second for his brain to catch up and realise exactly what he was looking at. Brian stood there holding his shirt up under his arms, proudly showing off the small bulge in his belly.

"Oh wow," Patrick said from behind him. "Can I touch?" Brian nodded happily and Patrick walked up and placed his hands on the small bump.

Marcus couldn't look any prouder. "He's been walking around since Tuesday showing it off to anyone that will look." Jake turned his attention once more to Patrick. The man looked genuinely happy for his brother and his mate.

After everything they had learnt while away Jake wondered if he would ever get the chance to feel his mate's stomach swollen with their child. Patrick turned at that moment and smiled at him causing Jake's heart to skip a beat at the pure happiness shining in his mate's face.

Zack and Simon walked in soon after followed by Hayley and the noise level seemed to increase around the table. Jake excused himself not long after to go shower and dress.

He'd just stepped into the water when he heard the

door to the bathroom open then close. He smiled at the thought of having his mate wet and naked in his arms. He turned to face the shower door and waited for his mate to join him.

He didn't have to wait long. The door opened and a very naked Patrick stepped up to him. "You forgot something."

"I did?" He asked not sure what Patrick was talking about now.

"Yep. Me. Oh, and this." Jake looked down as a bottle of lube was placed into his hand. He growled and lifted Patrick into his arms. Even though there were only a few inches in height separating them, Jake still loved the feeling of his mate's legs wrapped around him.

Patrick didn't disappoint, his ankles locked behind his back and his wrists did the same behind his neck. Patrick tugged his head down until their lips met in a scorching kiss. Jake stepped back until Patrick's back was against the wall. His mate moaned into his throat and thrust his hips, rubbing their hard cocks together.

"Please—" Patrick was so sexy when he begged. The man pulled his lips away then started attacking his jaw and neck, kissing and biting at the skin as he went.

Jake flicked the lid off the bottle of lube before

pouring the liquid over his fingers. He reached around and found the tight star he was looking for. Not waiting, Jake thrust two fingers into his mate's quivering hole. Patrick screamed his pleasure and bit down on his neck, his canines spearing Jake's skin. Thrusting his fingers quickly in and out of Patrick's hole he added a third before removing them altogether.

He poured more lube on to his hand before throwing the bottle away. Coating his shaft and grabbing Patrick's hips, Jake angled him until the head of his cock was resting against Patrick's tight entrance.

"Do it," Patrick panted at him. Jake thrust forward, burying himself balls deep in one smooth stroke, then pulling almost the entire way out and thrusting back in again. Patrick cried out and tried to thrust his hips back against Jake, attempting to bury his mate's cock even deeper.

Jake wasn't going to last long. He gripped Patrick's ass cheeks and pulled them apart, allowing him to thrust even farther. Patrick's mewling cries sent Jake over the edge as he pounded his mate into the shower wall. As the first spurts of cum shot from his cock he roared his climax and sank his canines into Patrick's neck, once again claiming his mate.

Patrick continued to ride his cock, screaming his delight when he followed Jake quickly into orgasm. The feel of Patrick's tight walls quivering and clamping down on his still hard shaft sent another spurt of seed into his mate's hungry hole. Jake collapsed against Patrick and moaned as he felt the mating knot extend and take hold.

Patrick whimpered in his arms, shuddering as his body was forced through another orgasm. Jake's mate lay panting in his arms, legs loosely wrapped around him, arms barely holding on. "Need sleep," Patrick moaned.

Jake laughed. "Sorry babe, but I don't think we're going to get any more of that at the moment." Patrick looked up at him, his eyes heavy lidded from his orgasm, his entire body relaxed and sated. Jake had never seen a more beautiful sight. He took his mate's lips in a slow leisurely kiss, teasing and tasting his love's mouth.

"Love you, Patrick," he murmured against his ear.

"Hmmm, love you too, Jay." Patrick rested in his arms, against the shower wall, until the knot receded. Jake missed the feeling of his mate as soon as his cock slid free but knew it wasn't practical to walk around all day with Patrick impaled on his cock no matter how much he might want to.

Patrick slid his legs down Jake's body until he once

again had his feet under him. They washed each other in relative silence, the pair of them both sporting happy, satisfied grins.

Jake turned the shower off when sure they were both clean and passed Patrick a towel as he stepped out. They dried and wandered into the bedroom to dress. If Jake planned on staying with Patrick here he would have to go home and grab some more clothes. The rest of his stuff he didn't really care about.

Grabbing a clean pair of jeans from his suitcase Jake pulled them on, not bothering with underwear. He then grabbed a blue shirt and pulled it over his head. A wolf whistle from behind him had him turning and blowing a kiss at his mate. Jake didn't think he had ever been this happy before. They left the bedroom hand in hand and found everyone had migrated to the living room.

Jake stopped dead when he also realised Patrick's parents had arrived. Maryanne got up right away and hurried over and gave him a hug and a kiss on the cheek. "I can't really welcome you to the family, as you've always been a member. But I hope you two will be happy together," she said patting his cheek.

She then kissed her son before going back to take her seat next to her husband.

Joe looked at him and Jake had a hard time not squirming under the intense gaze of his old Alpha. "Jake."

"Yes, sir?"

"Make sure you treat him right."

"I'll do everything in my power to make sure Patrick's always happy," Jake answered the older man. Joe seemed satisfied as he nodded and sat back, wrapping an arm around his wife's shoulders.

Jake scanned the rest of the occupants of the room and noticed both pack doctors were here. "Morning Doc, Doc," he said as he nodded to both of them. Stephanie Owens, the Leyburn pack doctor, was a short plump woman in her early forties. She was mated to the town mechanic and they had three young cubs. The other doc, Philip Carter, was a man in his late fifties with silver hair and stood just shy of six feet, Jake thought.

Once their hellos were issued, the pair went back to quietly discussing Brian's care in the months to come. Jake took the only seat available, the leather armchair next to the one Alex and Jason were currently sitting in. Patrick walked over and sat on the arm of the chair.

Jake shifted so he could touch his mate and happily settled with his hand rubbing circles across his mate's back, under his shirt.

Brian was sitting on his mate's lap, Marcus's hands gently rubbing his swollen belly. All eyes in the room however turned to them as they waited to find out what Patrick and Jake had learnt.

Jake recited all the information he could remember from the Pennaeth Alpha, anything he missed or forgot Patrick jumped in with. Once they had finished, the entire room looked back at them in silence.

"So only on the new moon?" Jason wanted to know eagerly.

"Yep, so can you go without for one night?" Patrick joked.

"Don't know, maybe. We'll have to wait and see." He laughed then looked thoughtful. "What about the months where there is no new moon?" he asked.

"I'd say you're safe. We were told only on the new moon so if there isn't one then you can't get pregnant. We can always ask Alpha Taylor if we want confirmation," Jake replied.

They sat and discussed everything for several hours until the doctors stood. "If you don't mind, we're going to take Brian to Stephanie's clinic. She has an ultrasound machine, so we can get a look at the baby and make sure everything's fine. It will also allow us to see just how far along he is," Dr Carter stated to the room.

Brian stood eagerly, followed by Marcus. Brian walked over to Maryanne and held out his hand. "We would be honoured if you would come with us."

Maryanne looked shocked before a smile broke out across her face. "I would love to." Brian helped her stand and the five of them made their way out of the house.

Alex patted Jason on the butt, asking him to stand. The tall Alpha then turned to Jake. "I think it's time we had that talk. Don't you, Jake?" It wasn't really a question so Jake just nodded and kissed Patrick on the cheek as he followed his friend to the study.

He wasn't surprised when Joe followed them in. Alex gestured to the couch against the wall. Jake and Joe took a seat while Alex grabbed one of the chairs from in front of the desk and swung it around until he was facing them.

Jake thought he would get the first word in before Alex got time to get angry again. "I want you to know that I have known Patrick's my mate since not long after he turned sixteen."

"What the hell, man? That's ten god damn years!" Okay so maybe Alex was still angry.

"I know exactly how long it's been, Alex. There

hasn't been a day gone by that didn't register the fact that I was living without my other half."

"Then why?" Joe asked, his voice much calmer than his son's. The man didn't seem angry at all, just curious.

"I only told Patrick the entire truth two nights ago." He looked at his friend before continuing. "Will you hear me out entirely before you punch me again?" Jake didn't really care, he deserved every hit for what he had put Patrick through, but he knew his mate would more than likely feel it and go after his brother, and that was something Jake didn't want.

"If I like my nuts where they are then I can't touch you. You're safe," Alex grumbled. He didn't look entirely happy at the admission.

"Patrick has lived with the knowledge of who his mate is for the last ten years and believed I didn't want him."

"Why the hell would he believe something like that?" Joe asked.

"Because that's what I told him." Jake waited for a minute before he continued his tale. He told them everything. All about how he had found out Patrick was his mate and his father's reaction to the news and finally about his late night phone call to Patrick.

"Jesus Christ," Alex said, running his hands though his hair.

"You denied your mate for ten years so you would keep my son safe?" Joe asked.

"Yes, sir. It was the only thing I could think of to do at the time. My father was the third strongest wolf in the pack and I believed one hundred per cent that he would carry out his threat if I claimed Patrick.

"I thought so long as I was at uni he was safe. When I finished and moved back here I vowed to watch over him, and make sure my dad kept his promise to not touch my mate. I started working out to gain strength, but these things take time. It was only when Alex became Alpha and I challenged for Beta that I realised I might be able to take my father in a fight. However it had been nearly eight years and I didn't think Patrick could ever forgive me for denying him for so long."

"Where's your father now?" Alex asked, his voice laced with fury.

"I have no idea. I've barely spoken to the man since that night."

"Don't worry, son, we'll find him and bring him to justice. Both you and Patrick will be safe." Jake nodded, but he didn't think it would be that easy. His father wouldn't go lying down. He was a stubborn old bastard and would fight the whole way.

"Love you." The words whispered though his mind and Jake couldn't help but smile.

"Love you too," he replied.

CHAPTER 10

Rick sat at the table with his brother Simon and his daughter Hayley while Zack and Jason puttered around the kitchen, organising lunch. He knew Alex and his dad were grilling Jake about their mating. He wanted to be in there defending his man but thought it best if he left everything up to Jake.

He understood why Jake had done what he had done. Yes, it hurt that they had missed out on so much time together, but if the roles were reversed he knew he would do anything to keep his mate safe. With Rick only being sixteen when everything happened, he couldn't begin to imagine how difficult the choice must have been for Jake.

Zack and Jason were just laying everything on the table for lunch when Alex walked in, followed by their dad and Jake. Rick jumped up and raced to his mate, throwing his arms around his neck and hugging him tight. "Hey there, everything's fine." Jake soothed him. He had no idea why he was acting so needy, but put it down to finally having a mate after so long.

They all took seats and started lunch. Half an hour later they heard the others arrive home. They all looked up as a beaming Brian bounced into the room holding pictures in his hand. Patrick kept watching as his smiling mother walked in next, followed by a very pale looking Marcus.

Brian was showing his dad the pictures. "Look, here's baby A and here's baby B." He was pointing at the paper in his hands. Joe looked shocked and silence descended on the table. "Twins?" Brian's smile got wider and the man started nodding enthusiastically.

Marcus however looked a little green around the gills. "You okay, bro?" Rick asked.

"Twins," his brother whispered.

"Oh, don't worry about him. He'll be fine in a minute. He fainted in the clinic, just needs some time for everything to sink in," their mother announced.

The room broke into sudden laughter at hearing of Marcus fainting because of a couple of little babies. Marcus sat at the table before he fell down. Brian made his way over and plopped down into his lap. Marcus's arms automatically went around his mate and started rubbing his belly. Brian sat there and hummed happily.

"So according to the docs I'm just over six weeks along. I'm showing already because there are two of them. It's still a little early to tell what sex they are though so that's going to be a surprise. Dr Carter stayed back with Stephanie to go over everything she'll need to know. He said he'd come back a week before I'm due to help her with the birth," Brian announced to the room.

Patrick didn't know about anyone else but he was still a little shocked about the whole twin thing. Glancing back at his brother, he was happy to note a healthier looking colour to his face.

Things soon settled down again around the table and everyone ate lunch and talked about the impending birth. Patrick's mum and dad left not long after, stating they had to get back home before Stephanie dropped Dr Carter back. After they left, Brian and Marcus excused themselves to go have some private time and absorb the news about their babies. Simon and Zack took Hayley to the park and Alex disappeared upstairs chasing after Jason.

Patrick led Jake back to the living room where they curled up together on the couch and watched the Saturday afternoon football game.

* * * *

Two days later found Jake sitting in his office going over what had happened in his cases while he'd been away last week. Jake startled when his mobile rang, shattering the quiet in his office. Glancing at the screen he saw it was

Alex calling.

"Hey man, what's up?"

"Your dad's missing." Alex's voice sounded gruff.

Jake sat up straight, wondering if he had heard his friend correctly. "Huh?"

"Dad and I went around to his house yesterday to have a word with him." Yeah, Jake could just imagine exactly what would have been said between the three. He smirked at the thought of his current and former Alpha going to pick up his dad so he could be brought before the pack. "Anyway, he wasn't home, there was no sight of him anywhere. We thought we could get him this morning at work, but apparently he quit last Monday and no one has seen him since."

"Shit, I don't like the sound of that," Jake growled. If his father got anywhere near Patrick, Jake would kill the miserable old bastard.

"Neither do I. I have Marcus checking for any sign of him through official channels but so far nothing."

"Thanks for letting me know." Why couldn't his dad just be happy for him and let him live his life?

"No worries, I'll see you tonight," Alex said then disconnected the call.

Shit! Well there wasn't anything Jake could do until

they found out where his father had disappeared to. It didn't stop him from worrying about his mate's safety though. He wondered if he could convince Patrick to take some more time off work until they caught up to his father. Somehow he didn't think so. Setting his worries aside for now Jake went back to work.

By four that afternoon Jake had conducted two meetings and a teleconference as well as completing a mile of paperwork and he was ready to call it a day. Packing up, he was about to leave when his mobile rang for what felt like the thousandth time that day.

He didn't recognise the number, but that wasn't unusual. "Hello, Jake Richmond," he answered on the fourth ring.

"You were warned, boy," his father said before hanging up.

Jake's heart rate just about doubled at the words. He grabbed his briefcase and raced out of the office, dialling Patrick's number as he ran. The phone in his ear rang several times before cutting to the message bank. Jake hung up and tried again.

"Come on, babe, answer the damn phone." But no luck, it cut to the message bank again after half a dozen rings. Jake swore as he pressed the button to cut the call.

Changing tactics, he dialled Alex.

Just as he got to his car, the call was answered. "Jake."

"Do you know where Patrick is?" Jake didn't have time for pleasantries. He needed to find his mate. Starting the car, Jake placed the call though the car's Bluetooth and took off for home.

"Why, what's happened?" Alex sounded alert all of a sudden.

"Dad called and Patrick's not answering his phone. I'm on my way home now."

"Fuck, I'll go check his work. Call me if you find him."

"Will do." Jake disconnected the call and pressed his foot that much harder on the accelerator. Five minutes later Jake screeched to a halt in front of Patrick's house. Jake was thankful to see his mate's car in the driveway but wouldn't breathe easier until he knew for a fact that his man was inside and safe.

He dialled Alex back as he ran up the lawn. As soon as Alex answered he informed his friend Patrick's car was at home then hung up. Jake opened the door with such force it slammed against the wall behind it.

"Patrick!" he yelled, but there was no answer. He

searched the living room, finding no one he continued to the kitchen where loud music was playing and he found Brian cooking. "Where's Patrick?" he asked anxiously over the noise.

Brian spun around, his hand lifting to cover his chest. "Shit, Jake! You scared the hell out of me."

"Have you seen Patrick?" he tried again.

"Yeah, about ten minutes ago. I think he said something about a shower." Jake nodded and ran for his room.

As soon as he opened the door he could hear the shower running. Silently thanking god that his mate was safe he stalked into the bathroom and opened the shower door just as Patrick turned the water off. Grabbing his mate by the wrist he pulled the sopping wet man into his arms.

Patrick let out a surprised yelp before he realised who held him and wrapped his arms around Jake's middle.

"Hey, what's wrong? You're trembling," Patrick asked quietly. Jake just shook his head, not being able to answer at that moment. He just needed to hold his mate.

"Shhh, I'm fine, everything's going to be okay." Before Jake could answer Patrick their bedroom door slammed open, followed by a heavy tread as Alex yelled out to him. "Jake?"

"In here, Alex. He's safe, I have him."

"Thank god," Alex said, relieved, as he walked into the bathroom.

"Hey, do you mind?" Patrick looked at his brother, affronted. It was only then that it registered that Patrick was wet and naked in his arms. Jake spun them around until he was sure Alex couldn't see anything of Patrick's nakedness. He looked at his friend and growled. No one got to see his mate naked but him.

Alex laughed and raised his hands. "Dude, seriously, eww, he's my brother." Jake just shook his head, it didn't matter to him. No one got to see Patrick naked. Alex just laughed again and left them alone.

"Want to tell me, now, what's going on?" Patrick asked as he rubbed his hands up and down Jake's back and kissed his stubbled chin.

"Dad's missing, no one has seen him in a week." Jake stopped, not wanting to tell his mate about the phone call he got.

"Okay then." Patrick looked sceptical. "I can understand why that would bother you but why was your heart just about racing out of your chest and your body trembling when you yanked me out of the shower?" His mate was far too intelligent for his own good.

Seeing no alternative to the truth, Jake sighed. "He called me as I was leaving the office. He told me I had been warned. I thought he had gotten you. I tried calling but you didn't answer. I feared the worst."

Patrick tightened his hold quickly before stepping back. He took a hold of Jake's hand and led them back to the bedroom. Jake stood still as Patrick moved his hands inside his jacket and slipped it from his shoulders. They left the jacket where it fell.

Jake's shirt quickly followed his jacket before Patrick started on his belt and suit pants' button and zipper, finally pushing them to the floor. Jake sat on the edge of the bed as Patrick knelt in front of him and removed his shoes, one by one. Once he was completely naked Jake shivered as his mate kissed his thighs. He continued to lay kisses on his legs as he worked his way closer to Jake's now straining length.

Jake moaned in pure pleasure as Patrick lapped at his furry balls before leaving them to take his cock into the warm recesses of his mouth. This was just what Jake needed. He needed to feel his mate, alive and under him. He needed to claim what was his.

Pulling Patrick from his cock, Jake flipped them on the bed until his mate lay under him, and Jake set about proving exactly who Patrick belonged to.

* * * *

Three weeks. It had been three weeks and they still hadn't heard a single peep out of Jake's father. The whole thing was starting to piss Rick off. Jake, Alex, and even his dad were keeping so close a watch on him Rick could barely take a piss without someone wanting to know where the hell he was going.

It was the night of the full moon and Alex would be announcing their mating to the rest of the pack tonight. It would be their first opportunity to run on their lands as a mated couple. With everything that had been going on, Jake hadn't thought it was safe enough for the pair of them to go for a run.

Rick's wolf was itching to get out and run on home soil. He was practically vibrating in his seat as they drove to the pack meeting. Jake reached over and rested a hand on his thigh, squeezing gently. "Calm down, babe, we'll be running before you know it."

"We better be," Rick grunted in reply. He had been feeling extremely caged over the last three weeks. Just because he understood why everyone was acting the way they were, didn't mean he had to like it. He didn't know how Brian was coping. Now well over halfway through his second trimester, it was fairly obvious the man was pregnant. As the baby bump couldn't possibly be mistaken for anything else, he was house bound so no humans would see his state. Brian seemed to be fine with the choice as his belly continued to swell bigger with the babes he carried.

Rick loved the idea of being a father, and creating a life with the man he loved filled his heart with joy at the thought. He just wasn't a hundred per cent sure he could handle being pregnant. The thought had never even entered his head until recently. It was definitely something they would need to discuss in the future. But for now Rick was happy with it being just the two of them.

Jake pulled the car into the nearly full car park and switched off the engine. Patrick had undone his seatbelt and jumped out of the car before Jake had removed the keys from the ignition. He waited, bouncing on the spot for Jake to join him.

Jake got out of the car laughing. "Come on, babe, let's go before you bounce away." He kissed Rick on the lips then took his hand and led the way through the bush. They emerged into the pack clearing a few minutes later. Jake and Rick made their way over to stand with the rest of his family.

A couple of pack members who had heard about their mating came and offered their congratulations before Alex started the meeting. An hour later Rick never thought he would be so happy to hear his brother stop talking. Rick stripped and watched as Jake did the same. He still had trouble sometimes believing the incredibly sexy man in front of him was all his.

Once they were both naked Rick quickly kissed his mate whispering in his ear, "See you on the dark side." He stepped back laughing and let the change take over. Seconds later he was standing on all fours and looking at a very large black wolf. Jake nipped his neck and licked his muzzle.

"Let's go, gorgeous. Time to run."

"Hell yeah!" Jake waited until Rick was by his side then they took off through the trees. They ran, hunted, and played together for hours before Jake led them to his favourite section of the large stream that ran though the pack lands. Rick had never had so much fun on a run in his life, and hunting with Jake was incredible due to their link.

Rick stopped to lap at the water, quenching his thirst from all his running. He would love to find a nice secluded spot where he and Jake could curl up together as wolves and rest. Jake joined him and they drank generously. A twig snapping had Rick turning around.

He crouched down and growled as Arthur Richmond stepped out from behind a tree. Rick's hackles rose as he noticed the gun pointing directly at him. Jake snapped his jaws at his father and took a step closer to the other man.

"Uh-uh, Jake. If you think you can get to me before I can shoot your mate, then by all means try." Jake's father had a crazy gleam in his eyes and Rick had a bad feeling someone was going to get hurt. He hoped to Christ it wasn't going to be them.

"Jake, please don't do anything stupid. The man has a gun," Rick begged his mate.

Jake didn't answer him, instead he edged closer and closer to Rick.

"I warned you about what would happen if you claimed Patrick. All you had to do was stay away from him. Why couldn't you have mated a nice female and had a couple of cubs?" he asked as he waved the gun back and forth. Rick thought the man sounded slightly insane, but he didn't really know Arthur Richmond very well so he wasn't the best judge.

Jake bared his teeth and growled at his father. His

back legs tensed as if he was ready to leap at any moment.

"I always keep my promises," Arthur said as his back straightened and he took aim.

Both Rick and Jake leapt at the man, Rick only slightly behind his mate. The gun went off, the sound reverberating through the silent clearing. Rick watched in horror as his mate fell in front of him. He saw Arthur Richmond standing stunned, looking at his son before he turned and looked at Rick, hate in his eyes.

Rick wasn't about to let the man get a second shot off. He covered the remaining distance between them quickly and leapt, taking his target to the ground. He clamped his jaws around the older man's throat before he'd even realised what had happened. Jake's father dropped the gun in his surprise and attempted to pry him off.

Not giving up, Rick stood and applied more pressure shaking his head until he heard a distinct snap. Stepping back, Rick turned and headed for his mate. He knew Jake lived as he could still feel their bond alive and crackling between them.

He crouched low on his belly and scooted forward until he was as close to Jake as he could be. He licked at the blood he could see matting his mate's fur. Rick lifted his head and howled to the rest of his pack. Help would come soon, his mate simply too large for Rick to be able to carry by himself. He settled down to guard his mate against any other predators that might think to hurt him.

* * * *

Jake woke to pain and a swaying motion. He tilted his head, then realised several things all at once. One, he was still in wolf form, two, his father had shot him and, three, he was being carried by his Alpha.

"Hang on, buddy, we're nearly there." Alex's deep voice rumbled.

Jake, however, needed to find his mate. What the hell had happened after he'd been shot? Where were Patrick, and his father? Please don't tell him Patrick had been hurt too. Jake started to struggle in Alex's hold. He cried out, which came out as more a whimper in his current form when he moved wrong.

Alex must have understood what he needed though as his next words managed to calm him like nothing else. "Jake lie still, you're heavy enough as it is. Patrick is fine. He's following behind me, still in wolf form. We'll be at the clearing in a minute and Doc can take a look at you."

Jake closed his eyes and tried to ignore the pain

radiating through his body. Being a shifter helped incredibly on cutting down his healing time. However, until they got the bullet out of his body, Jake would remain in constant pain and he would have to stay in his wolf form. He couldn't risk shifting with the object still in his body. God only knew where it would end up with all the changes his form went through to get back to human. Once the bullet was removed Jake could shift and start the healing process.

Before he knew it they were back at the clearing and Alex was laying Jake on the ground. Patrick edged closer until he was right beside him. Jake lifted his head carefully and licked at his mate's muzzle. *"I'm fine, babe. I'll be back to normal by the morning, just you wait and see."*

"You bloody better be. Don't you ever do this again. I just got you back in my life, I'm not ready to lose you yet."

"I hadn't planned on it. It'll take a hell of a lot more than a mere bullet to separate me from you now." Patrick huffed down their link, but he could tell the man wasn't really mad, more scared and worried. He didn't blame him. When Jake had seen his father pointing a gun directly at his mate, he didn't think he'd been so shit scared in his life.

"What happened to my father?" he asked.

"Sorry," Patrick replied softly. He could feel the conflicting emotions practically pouring off his mate and knew what Patrick had been forced to do. He hated his dad even more in that instant for what he had forced his mate to do to protect them.

"It's okay, babe, he deserved to die, and now we're safe to live our lives together." Jake couldn't help but feel overwhelming love and happiness at that prospect.

Before he could say anything else to his mate, Doc Stephanie came rushing up to them with a medical bag in hand. She collapsed to the ground on the other side of Jake and pulled out a scalpel. Patrick took one look at the implement and bared his teeth then growled at the Doc.

Only then did Stephanie realise there was a slightly protective wolf hovering over her patient. Jake thought it was hot as hell when Patrick got all protective and possessive. Patrick's mother on the other hand had different feelings. She cuffed him across the back of his head before admonishing him.

"Stop being so difficult and let the woman do her job. The sooner she gets the bullet out, the sooner Jake can shift." Patrick dropped his head at the dressing down and lowered himself to his belly. Jake thought he was cute and licked his muzzle again.

"This might hurt." Jake had barely registered the words before there was sharp pain where she had cut to re-open the already healing wound followed by what felt like a pair of hot pokers being plunged into his skin.

She seemed to dig around for god damn ever before giving a triumphant sound and her hand pulled back holding the offending bullet between the end of a pair of what looked suspiciously like tweezers. Jake could have sworn the damn things felt like they were the size of fire pokers.

Immediate relief swamped his body as he shifted back to human form. The throbbing pain radiating from his right shoulder joint had changed to a dull ache. By morning it would be gone altogether. Seconds after Jake was back to human form again, he found himself with an armful of naked mate.

Patrick was wriggling around on top of him kissing every part of his face he could reach. Jake felt himself grow hard at the friction Patrick caused as he moved his body back and forth then side to side.

Jake reached up and grabbed Patrick's hips, stilling the man where he lay. "If you don't stop moving I'm going to take you right here and now, no matter who's watching," Jake promised his man. Patrick seemed to stop breathing for a second as he lifted his head and looked around at the smiling faces of his entire family. He then flushed an adorable shade of red and buried his head in Jake's neck.

Everyone surrounding them broke into laughter before they all headed off in their own directions. Jake slapped Patrick on the ass. "Come on, babe, let's go home."

Patrick lifted his head, his smile shining brighter than the sun at high noon. "You have no idea how long I've waited for you to say that."

Jake had an idea. With his father now gone his mate was no longer forbidden and Jake planned to make the most of that. He couldn't wait to see what the years ahead held for him and his mate.

EPILOGUE

Two months later

Alex woke from a dead sleep, groggy and wondering what the hell could have woken him in the middle of the night. Jason was still fast asleep, snuggled tight in his arms. Alex rubbed his hand up and down his mate's back. He loved the feel of Jason in his arms. From the first night Jason had arrived in their home and knocked on Alex's door, there hadn't been a single night that they had slept apart. Jason had come a long way considering everything he had been through and Alex couldn't have been prouder of his mate.

Yes, Jason still occasionally had nightmares, but they were becoming further apart as time went by. Alex's hand wandered farther down Jason's smooth, silky skin until his hand gently cupped Jason's ass. Alex's cock perked right up, he figured since he was awake he might as well have a little fun. His fingers slipped into the warmth of Jason's crack and he tapped against the tight entrance he loved so much.

Jason moaned in his sleep and pushed back against his fingers. Alex loved that no matter what state Jason was in, his body always sought out his touch. He pushed a little harder and felt his finger slip right in to the welcome warmth of Jason's body, happy that Jason was still lubed up from the encounter earlier that night.

The sounds Jason made as he continued to sleep drove Alex's cock to aching hardness. Pushing in with a second finger Alex crooked his finger until he found just what he was looking for. Jason pushed back harder against his invading fingers and Alex watched as Jason's eyes fluttered open.

"Mmm… wanting something?"

"You know me, Sweetheart, I'll never get enough of your sexy body." Alex rolled them over until he had Jason under him. He had just slipped his fingers out and lined his cock up when a scream rent the air.

"What the hell?" Jason asked as he sat upright, pushing at Alex's chest. Frustrated as hell, Alex got out of bed and grabbed the jeans he had been wearing yesterday and jammed his still hard cock into the pants. Once he and Jason were covered they made their way out of the room.

Alex could hear noises coming from Marcus and Brian's room. When another scream broke the air Alex didn't even bother knocking, he opened the door and made his way into his brother's bedroom. He took everything in within an instant. Brian, breathing heavily, standing at the end of the bed leaning over, one arm trying to take his weight as his other arm rubbed his extremely large, distended stomach. Marcus stood behind him in nothing but sleep pants rubbing his back, whispering soothing words to his mate.

"Everything okay?" Alex asked

"Contractions started about an hour ago. They're getting stronger and closer together," Marcus answered him. "We need to get him to mum and dad's. Can you call them and give them a heads up?" Alex nodded as he left the room looking for his phone. Dr Carter had arrived a week ago, and together with Stephanie Owens, their pack doctor, they had set up a temporary clean room in their parents' house, where Brian could deliver the twins.

Alex couldn't wait for the babies to be born. He loved having Hayley running around the house. Jason and he had started talking about having children of their own, but Alex was more than happy to wait until Jason was ready.

Walking into his bedroom Alex picked his phone up from the bedside table where he had left it and dialled their parents to give them and Dr Carter a heads up that they were about to be bombarded with people.

* * * *

Rick sat cuddled up in Jake's lap in his parents' living room. Rick decided that being woken by a scream is probably one of the worst ways possible to wake up. Simon and Zack had stayed home so they didn't have to wake their daughter, Hayley. They would be around as soon as she was up. Everyone else though had piled into cars and headed to his parents.

The lights had been on as they all had pulled up to his parents' house and his mum and dad were standing out front waiting for them. Rick had watched as Marcus got out of the car Alex had driven and picked a very heavily pregnant Brian up in his arms and walked with purpose towards the house. Marcus waited while his mother kissed him on the cheek before bending and kissing Brian.

Rick, Jake, Alex and Jason all followed along behind and entered the house. They all headed straight for the kitchen and the lure of coffee, except Jason who settled for a glass of juice. Coffee cups in hand they decided to wait in comfort and walked back through the house to the living room.

Now nearly two hours later they still sat here waiting. Rick's mum and dad had joined them not long after they had all settled down, deciding it was best to leave things to the professionals. Rick had dozed on and off, comfortable in his mate's arms. The last two months had been the happiest of his life. Jake had moved in with him with surprisingly little argument. Rick had thought that Jake would want to keep his unit and for them to live together there. He was pleased this was not the case. He knew one day all the brothers would branch out and get their own places, but at the moment Rick liked things the way they were.

He wasn't kidding himself though. He knew adding two newborn babies into the mix was going to create a few sleepless nights, but they were family and honestly Rick was looking forward to getting to hold his little nieces or nephews in his arms. He couldn't wait to have kids of his own one day, but for now he and Jake were still settling into their newly mated lives together.

* * * *

Marcus had felt helpless as he stood by and watched his mate in pain. Brian had woken him when the contractions had started. He hated to see his mate in any sort of pain but he was unable to do anything to relieve the pressure put on his body. Now hours later Brian was drugged and lying on a surgical bed with a screen placed over his middle so they couldn't see what the doctors were doing.

Marcus sat by Brian's head, running his fingers through his mate's beautiful hair. He leant forward and kissed Brian.

"You're doing so well, baby. I love you. Just a little longer and you'll be able to hold our children in your arms." Marcus kept his voice soft, soothing, he couldn't even begin to imagine everything Brian was thinking and feeling at the moment.

Brian turned his head to look at him. His eyes alight with both excitement and worry. Marcus ignored the quiet conversations taking place between the doctors and concentrated solely on Brian. "Everything's going to be fine. I'm so proud of you."

"Next time, it's your turn," Brian whispered to him. Marcus laughed—joy filling his soul. His laugh was cut short suddenly by a small cry from behind the curtain. Marcus heard Brian's indrawn breath as they both turned to stare at the curtain between them and the noise.

Stephanie stepped from behind the material holding a small crying baby. Marcus felt shock first at the sight of his child then overwhelming love. This was his and Brian's cub. "Congratulations dads, it's a boy!" Marcus heard Brian sob beside him as he looked at his child. The small boy was wrinkled, his face was red from crying and his entire body was covered in goop, but Marcus was sure he had never seen a better sight other than his mate. Stephanie quickly took the baby away to clean and wrap before handing him to Marcus and disappearing back behind the curtain to deliver baby number two.

Marcus placed the baby gently on Brian's chest, he thought it was only fair that Brian got a cuddle as he had been the one to carry them for the last five months. Marcus wiped the tears from Brian's face and kissed his mate on the forehead as Brian gently stroked the small bundle on his chest.

"You did so good, baby. Look at him, he's gorgeous."

"He has your eyes," Brian said to him. Marcus nodded. The Holland genes were strong in his family with nearly every child being born having brown eyes and his son was no different.

"Welcome to the world, little Samuel Joseph," Marcus said before kissing his son on the head. He and Brian had talked for hours about what they were going to call their children. Knowing they were having twins but not knowing the sexes made things even more difficult as they had to come up with four names, two boy's and two girl's.

Brian had agreed wholeheartedly when he said he would like to include his parents' names if possible. Marcus was snapped out of his thoughts by another baby's cry. Looking down at the small sleeping form on Brian's chest he realised his second child had just been born.

Marcus waited anxiously for Stephanie to introduce them to their child. He squeezed Brian's hand as the woman finally walked towards them with their second baby. "It's another boy, gentlemen," she announced with a huge grin. Marcus had to admit he was a little relieved. He loved Hayley to death but he wasn't sure he would have known what to do with a girl. Maybe a little further down the track.

From the quick glimpse he'd gotten of his son before Stephanie took him away to clean him up, he thought the boys looked exactly the same. Stephanie came back and handed his son to him. Marcus was so scared he would drop this tiny precious baby. He would have to get used to this daddy business. He leant down and whispered in Brian's ear, "Thank you."

Brian smiled at him but the smile slowly faded and he whispered softly, "I think I'm going to throw up."

Marcus immediately sat up straight and quickly grabbed a bowl with his baby-free hand. The doctors had placed it there earlier, telling them it was a common occurrence after the birth.

When Brian's stomach finally settled, he relaxed back on the bed, his eyes closing as he let sleep take over. Stephanie walked over to them and picked Sammy up and deposited him in Marcus's other arm. "Why don't you go introduce your sons to your family and let us finish up here?" Marcus nodded, in a daze as he was led to the door. The doctors closed the door firmly behind him and he suddenly felt the full weight of fatherhood on his shoulders. After taking a deep breath, he headed towards the living room to introduce the newest members of his family.

* * * *

Simon and Zack had stayed behind to let Hayley sleep. Seeing as how they were awake and had the house to themselves, Simon had taken the opportunity to drive his mate wild and make him scream. Now standing in the shower with his wet, soapy mate, Simon was wondering if they had time for another round before their daughter woke.

Zack pulled off the 'just fucked' look very well. His body was still flushed and boneless from orgasm and his eyes hooded. He leant against Simon and moaned as he ran his soapy hands over his mate's body, washing his soft skin. Just when Simon had decided to start round two, he heard their daughter moving around in the bedroom.

Simon had never been happier than when Zack and Hayley had come into his life. Even though their private time was interrupted by their daughter on occasion, Simon wouldn't trade a minute of it.

"Let's go get our girl ready and then see if Brian has had the babies yet," Simon said to Zack then kissed his mate passionately. Zack nodded when they broke apart, his poor mate looked a little dazed, and Simon thought he'd never looked better.

Once everyone was dressed and Hayley had eaten a quick slice of toast for breakfast, they all piled into the car and headed for his folks' place.

Simon didn't bother knocking as he led his small family into the house. They found everyone in the living room, Hayley ran right to his mother for cuddles. Simon realised they hadn't missed the main event yet since they were still waiting on news.

He sat down in one of the available chairs and pulled Zack down on to his lap. No matter how long he lived he would never get tired of holding his mate in his arms.

* * * *

Maryanne sat anxiously waiting with her husband and sons for the birth of her grandcubs. Each one of her four strong boys had found their soul-mate and Maryanne couldn't be happier. Her family had now grown to include four extra sons and three grandcubs, just as soon as these two were born.

The room was quiet as they waited for news, they had heard cries coming from the room what seemed like hours ago but was probably only minutes. Maryanne let out a gasp and covered her mouth when she spotted Marcus walking towards them holding his cubs.

Everyone stood as they waited for Marcus to reach them. The smile on his face was radiant. Maryanne had only seen her son look this happy when Brian was by his side.

She watched as a tear trickled down her son's face and his voice caught in his throat as he tried to talk. "I would like to introduce you to our new sons. This is Samuel Joseph, he was born first." Marcus slightly lifted the baby in his left arm to indicate which cub he was talking about. "And this little one in Dylan Xander." He lifted the other arm. Both cubs where sleeping at the moment, but Maryanne knew they wouldn't stay that way for long, they never did.

"Would you like to hold your grandcubs, mum?" Marcus asked. Maryanne stepped forward nodding her head. She didn't think she was capable of speech at the moment. She gently took Dylan from Marcus's arms and watched as he handed Samuel to her husband.

"You did good, son," Joe murmured as he held the small baby in his arms.

"Don't look at me. Brian did all the hard work. The man deserves a medal as far as I'm concerned. Although he did tell me it was my turn next." The room broke out in hushed laughter as they tried not to wake the babies. Maryanne beamed as Marcus was congratulated by her other sons and their mates.

"How's Brian?" she asked.

"He's okay. He made it through the deliveries perfectly before he threw up and passed out from exhaustion."

Twenty minutes later the doctors came to join them in the living room and let Marcus know Brian was still sleeping and should heal relatively quickly from the surgery. He should be able to take him home by tonight.

Maryanne looked at her husband and smiled. The smile was returned. Even after all this time the man still did it for her. To see her sons grown and starting families of their own made her extremely proud of the men they had become. It didn't matter what the future held for their large family because this was what it was all about. Family. As long as they all stuck together they could get through anything.

ALSO BY AUTHOR

Available at **Silver Publishing**:

THE HOLLAND BROTHERS
Unexpected Mate
Determined Mate
Protective Mate
Forbidden Mate

25 DAYS OF CHRISTMAS
My Christmas Present

What Queer Magazine Online Says About Unexpected Mate:

Unexpected Mate is the first in a new werewolf shifting series from Toni Griffin. Set amongst smaller towns in what appeared to me to be a more rural backdrop gives it a special charm. I also enjoyed how Tori writes the brothers all living together yet separate from Mum and Dad. This gives another layer to the story that is almost a bit "boys gone wild", yet creates a wonderful sense of pack and camaraderie.

Marcus is a wolf determined not to be gay, so therefore he mustn't be. Dating female members of the pack and sleeping with them only confirms that, right? Wrong. The abrupt about face from denial to acceptance is well written, playing true to form as his brother's step forward to provide a much needed dose of reality. Marcus is a protective character, showing intensity with all emotions, but also displaying a fun-loving side. This fun-loving edge is the perfect foil for Brian.

When we first meet Brian, he has been exiled from his own pack. I connected with him quite quickly. Empathy was a powerful motivator as feelings of misplaced trust, trepidation, resentment and a basic feeling of fed up mix together in a volatile package. Brian shows true depth of emotion as the plot line develops. Contentment, tenderness and a side order of cheeky are the result, making Brian a very likeable character.

It is obvious there will be further instalments to this series and I, for one, can't wait to read them. I would recommend this story to anyone who enjoys shape-shifter or paranormal stories written in a contemporary style.

—Written by Nerine Petros

CPSIA information can be obtained at www.ICGtesting.com
Printed in the USA
BVOW032219300512

291420BV00003B/9/P

9 781614 953555